THE SENTIENT SPACE

IS THERE ANYONE OUT THERE?

THE SENTIENT SPACE

IS THERE ANYONE OUT THERE?

Edited by Kris Cotter

Stories by:
Lori Wilkey	Natashja Maccormick	Kay Hanifen
Megan Mackie	C.W. Stevenson	Jay Mendell
Courtney M. Privett	Rosalind Weir	Lou Kemp

4 Horsemen
Publications, Inc.

The Sentient Space: Is There Anyone Out There? Log Entry 2
Copyright © 2024 4 Horsemen Publications. All rights reserved.

4 Horsemen
Publications, Inc.

4 Horsemen Publications, Inc.
1497 Main St. Suite 169
Dunedin, FL 34698
4horsemenpublications.com
info@4horsemenpublications.com

Edited by Kris Cotter

Library of Congress Control Number: 2023944909

Print ISBN: 979-8-8232-0295-4
Ebook ISBN: 979-8-8232-0294-7

Dedication

To everyone that has stood and stared up at the stars.

Table of Contents

Introduction

Space, that final frontier, the great unknown, that vacuum in which no one can hear you scream, is that infinity and beyond which many believe must contain lifeforms that we could never comprehend, has drawn the attention of humanity for as long as we have been writing, and drawing, our stories. Looking up at the night sky, with its billions of twinkling, dancing lights, invokes feelings of wonderment and mystery. Even the youngest among us know that the secrets of the universe are laid out before us, begging us to explore and discover them.

The more we discover about space, the more we realize we don't know anything about it. We can't help but wonder whether the "cold dark" that we see is a void in space or a being that we can't see. As we ask questions, we apply our knowledge of life as it is here on our pale blue marble to create possible answers. Is the life out there friendly? Is it humanoid? Or is it a complex series of "vines" that control the minds of those physical creatures it comes into contact with slowly draining their life force until they are but a shell of their being?

Perhaps the questions that we are really searching for answers to are the ones about the problems we face here on Earth. Do other planets and civilizations struggle with "civil disobedience" and factions that think that all technology is "techno babble?" There has to be more out there than selfish, angry, violence, doesn't there? Not all other forms of life have to have wars that lead to "forbidden wastes," mass destruction, environmental decay, and great extinctions.

We, as a species, are looking for that small glimmer of hope in that light at the end of the cosmic tunnel, or in that silver lining on a star dust cloud floating in the vast darkness that out there, somewhere, are civilizations that are peaceful, happy, content, insert other positive word here. We aren't hoping to find a "self-serve party" free for all in our travels, but wouldn't it be amazing to find out that life isn't all about the survival of the fittest, kill or be killed, eat the weak, work every day until you die existence we have all come to know?

What if everything we think we know about life is wrong? Are there machines out there that keep the living alive, or perhaps contain life within themselves? How do the living entities around the universe get around? Do they fly through the air using wings or plane-like contraptions? Maybe we will stumble across a "railroad" that connects different planets and different systems and we will see things that are beyond the scope of human imagination.

We may never find the answers to all the questions that the infinite expanse of space begs us to ask, but we can have hope that one day, we may uncover a few of the innumerable secrets it holds. Or, this entire anthology could just be a "eulogy of an empty stargate."

Who knows...

Kris Cotter

Self-Serve Party

By Lori Wilkey

Baeznor glanced at his date, Zyphira. He appreciated the way her eyes sparkled in the moonlight as he piloted the borrowed cruiser. The Earth's Moon hovered so close to the window that he felt he could reach out and retrieve some moondust. He would give it to the prettiest girl in the universe. She currently sat beside him.

Baeznor studied Zyphira with one eye while gazing at the moon with the second eye, and with the third, he focused on the rapidly approaching planet.

Zyphira looked around the interior of the cruiser. "Do you always travel with a picture of your female progenitor on the instrument panel? Or do you keep it there because the color of her suckers matches the lights?" She didn't look impressed.

Explanations whirled through his brains. *Which sounds the best?* He hoped his glands weren't emitting any odors signaling his nervousness.

Finally settling on one explanation, he said, "I'm borrowing it from my progenitor while I wait for mine." *Phew, not a lie. She doesn't need to know that I haven't acquired one.*

Feeling clever, he took one tentacle off the controls and placed it on one of Zyphira's. Her multicolored eyes appraised him. After a few moments, he felt her relax and wrap her tentacle around his. He felt his insides turn to goo at her closeness.

"You know, my progenitor is an anthropologist. He's told me stories about this planet and some of the best places to go to obtain the true Earth experience. I can't wait to share them with you," Baeznor said. He attempted to hide the nervousness conveyed by his tentacles.

The tiny ship jounced as they entered the atmosphere. Baeznor's suckers quivered as his stomachs did flip-flops. He retrieved his tentacle from Zyphira with a grin that he hoped didn't look too queasy. It wouldn't do for Zyphira to know that he was new to space travel.

He brought the cruiser down outside of a small-size town. Reaching underneath the control panel, one of his tentacles rifled about, finally encountering a switch. When he flipped it, a low-grade hum whirred through the vehicle. The viewport wavered as the re-imaging shield engaged. "I've disguised our cruiser to look like a standard Earth vehicle," he explained.

The teen rummaged in a storage compartment, shoving assorted Earth artifacts out of the way. Zyphira peered over his tentacle, commenting about the objects. "Ooo, what is that?" she asked, pointing to an artifact that was two small, darkly translucent discs connected to each other with a tiny piece of wire. Slightly longer wires stuck out on either side of the flat discs.

"That's a laser inhibitor. The humans place them over their vision orifices to prevent lasers from shooting out."

Zyphira covered her mouth in delighted horror. "Is it safe for us to be here?"

"Sure! Only a few have the lasers. My progenitor showed me a human document with pictures of surgery done to their vision orifices. I can translate a few words of their language, but the pictures were explicit."

While searching in the storage cabinet above Zyphira's seat, Baeznor leaned close to her; his olfactory organ smelled her pungent stench. The suckers on the tip of his tentacle quivered with excitement. *At least she is too distracted to see my attraction.*

"I found it!" His triumphant voice echoed in the confined space. He held a small, computerized box in his tentacle. Baeznor's tentacle pushed a couple of buttons. "This will cast a re-imaging shield over anyone of our species within 10 meters of the box."

"I'll just have to stay close to you," said Zyphira, leaning closer to him.

"We look like humans now. How do I look?" he asked her.

"Hideous!"

Baeznor smirked, started up the vehicle again, then headed toward town. They drove past a thinning forest that gave way to fenced-in fields. The cruiser crept along. The slow speed allowed them to observe the native inhabitants.

They spotted a brown four-legged, two-headed animal contained within the enclosure. Fur covered the lower part of the body, including the lower elongated head. Fabric wrapped the upper half of the animal. This appeared to be a good idea to Baeznor, since he could see no fur on the upper portion of the creature except for the top of its head. The animal ran around in large circles, occasionally jumping over small obstacles. They heard strange sounds coming from the lower head.

"Neigh!"

The teens looked at each other, then back at the beast.

"What is it?" Zyphira asked in wonder.

"It must be a human-animal hybrid. See?" Baeznor pointed to the odd creature. "That top half looks humanoid."

Zyphira agreed.

The two tourists then continued their sightseeing at a crawl.

As they approached the town, more vehicles joined them on the roadway. The commotion outside the cruiser grew. Loud blasts emanated from the transportation conveyances behind them.

"What is that noise?" Zyphira asked, her ear stalks twitching.

"They are giving us a standard Earth greeting," Baeznor informed her. "They are a fascinating species. My progenitor told me many stories about them." Here Baeznor continued with human trivia, hoping to strike a knowledgeable tone. "Did you know that they willingly jump into enormous holes in the ground filled with water? They then traverse from one side of the hole to the other and back again, never seeming to find a way out." They both pondered the absurdity of these inhabitants.

They continued toward town, marveling at all the unique sights. Human vehicles continued to greet them the entire way. A smattering of buildings sprouted near the roadway. Humans strolled beside the road, a few alone, some in pairs, others in groups.

"The inhabitants seem to be friendly," Zyphira observed. Almost all the natives pointed and waved in their direction.

Baeznor guided the disguised cruiser over to a nearby building. He stopped in front of the building's large windows. "Let's explore a little."

"If you think it's safe," Zyphira undid her seat restraint and bumbled out of the cruiser. Baeznor hurried behind, never letting her from his sight.

"Look! That's what our cruiser looks like." They both peered at the reflection in the window. The tube-shaped vehicle was a riot of muted color. Painted flowers haphazardly decorated the body. A large "VW" glyph graced the front below the window. Rust flaked off from several worn patches.

Zyphira tilted her head as she evaluated their vehicle. Finally, a satisfied smile spread across her face. "Very human."

They wobbled as they walked. Neither had yet acclimated to Earth's gravity.

Zyphira attempted to walk straight forward but instead toppled into what she thought to be a human male.

"Sl- slorry," she slurred, her mouth not familiar with human speech. She placed her tentacle, which the re-imager disguised as a human hand, onto their cruiser.

"Don't you think it's a bit early to be drinking?" the human laughed. "You look about as trashed as your ride."

Confused, Zyphira glanced at Baeznor. He smiled at her and bobbed his head.

"Yes. Our ride is very trashed. Thank you. Just another ordinary Earth transportation conveyance," Baeznor said, patting the cruiser.

"Dude!" said another human to the first. "They are out there! That hippie van of theirs suits them. Let's go."

Baeznor leaned over to Zyphira and whispered, "Did you hear that? He liked our vehicle! They liked us! We passed as human!"

Gaining their Earth footing, the visitors ambled toward the building. Victory fueled their steps. Observing through the windows, the teens watched humans meandering amongst shelves containing Earth items. Individuals picked objects up and walked over to a computerized machine and waved the items over a square glass plate. Then the humans stuck a plastic card into a box for a few seconds. After retrieving their card, they exited the building. The visitors did not observe an attendant. The humans conducted all transactions in silence.

"We have seen that the humans can be quite boisterous. Think about how enthusiastically they greeted us. Perhaps they are not perm tted to speak inside the building," noted Baeznor.

"That seems like a good deduction."

Baeznor's stomachs gurgled. "I'm feeling depleted. What about you?"

Zyphira nodded, then asked, "But where do we attain sustenance?" She swept her human-looking arm toward the building in front of them.

They looked toward the building beside the one they currently faced. They saw a sign perched atop a tower of round rubber tubes next to a large grease-streaked door.

"Somewhere here," he indicated the sign.

Michelin Tires

"I can't decipher the entire thing, but my progenitor told me that first glyph refers to high-quality sustenance. The second glyph must refer to a type of nourishment, but I don't know what kind."

The two alien teens turned away from the building. They saw rectangular metal tanks with a black hose attached to the right side in the paved lot in front of the building. They looked remarkably like the nourishment tubes back home. Baeznor and Zyphira made their way over to the tanks, wobbling between the slowly moving vehicles. More humans delivered enthusiastic greetings.

"Humans are strange creatures," Zyphira said. "Look how they bring their vehicles with them to the nourishing tubes."

Baeznor laughed with her.

"I don't see any servers. It must be self-serve," Zyphira observed.

With a gallant sweep of his human-looking arm, he picked up a hose. "Allow me."

"How thoughtful you are."

He held the nozzle to Zyphira's mouth. When he pulled the trigger, liquid gushed into Zyphira's mouth and into her empty stomachs. Baeznor sensed the attention of the nearby humans. He looked away from his lovely date, despite her bizarre human appearance, and saw the locals pointing toward them. Human mouths opened wide and harsh noises spewed out. The high decibels made his ear stalks twitch. *This must be how the humans greet visitors outside of their vehicles.* He opened his mouth and imitated the human clamor to the best of his ability. He waved and turned his attention back to Zyphira.

Once she had had her fill, Baeznor took his turn at the nourishment center. Some liquid dribbled down his chin. Embarrassed, his limbs twitched. He used his camouflaged tentacle to wipe his face clean.

"Don't concern yourself. It's difficult to not make a mess using these dispensers. Ours are designed for our anatomy. These, not so much. Besides, look at what the crazy humans are doing with this sustenance."

Baeznor and Zyphira observed the humans place the hose into an opening of their vehicles, then depress the trigger and wait while the nourishment flowed into their vehicles. They replaced the hoses onto the tanks and departed.

"How silly these humans are! Why washte," Zyphira hiccupped. "Excuse me. Why waste something- *hic*- something, so tashty on a... on a vehicle? Wow! This liquid is powerful!"

By this time, a small crowd had gathered around the disguised aliens. Several individuals raised small handheld devices in their direction. A couple held these same devices to their ears. A discordant cacophony assaulted the teens' ear stalks.

"This musht be what is called a 'party.' My pro- *hic*- my progenitor told me about these; loud noise, losht of humans crowded together, and tashty sustenance," Baeznor slurred. "He also said that it ish polite to gyrate when attending a party."

The aliens staggered closer to the encroaching humans. The liquid that the visitors had ingested rapidly affected their systems. They twirled and whirled, stumbled, and careened. They chortled and surrendered to the festive atmosphere.

After imbibing at this Michelin nourishment center, Baeznor lacked inhibitions. He retrieved the re-imager from his pocket; it looked nearly identical to the devices the humans held. Wanting to blend in, he mimicked the humans and held it high. Then he grabbed Zyphira and swirled her around.

In the background, blaring, high-pitched whines added to the cacophony. Distant flashing red and white lights contributed to the sense of revelry. The humans pointed at the teens and laughed. Encouraged, Baeznor spun with his date faster.

Suddenly, he tripped, unable to understand Earth's gravity in his current state of mind. The re-imager flew out of his tentacle, smacking a human on the tip of its olfactory organ. The human rubbed its organ while stepping forward. The human's foot, encased in heavy rubber and leather, crushed the re-imager.

Baeznor and Zyphira's human images flickered and disappeared. Their tentacles no longer restrained, they gyrated with reckless abandon. Their six leg tentacles moved in intricate steps. Eventually, they noticed profound silence. The humans stared, mouths agape.

A wail pealed out of a human's mouth. Then pandemonium ensued. Humans shouted and ran in various directions. Several individuals hopped into their personal transportation devices and sped away. The human operating the vehicle closest to Baeznor and Zyphira departed so quickly, it forgot to replace the nourishment hose. Fluid spurted out from the nozzle, dowsing the ground and the two aliens. Within moments, the teens stood alone.

"I guess the party's over, *hic*." Zyphira swayed on her tentacles. "We should probably go home. My stomachs are rumbly. I don't think my system is ushed to such fancy nour- hic- nourishment."

"I'm so sorry!" Baeznor blurted in a panic. *I hope this doesn't mean that she won't go out with me again.* He placed a tentacle on hers and guided her toward the cruiser.

"Don't be! This wash the best first date ever!"

A long red vehicle accompanied by a couple of noisy blue and white vehicles, all with brilliant party lights rotating atop their roofs, arrived as Baeznor and Zyphira entered their cruiser.

"Don't forget to secure your restraints," Baeznor reminded Zyphira, the inebriating effects of their sustenance now rapidly dissipating. "Since the re-imager broke, they know we are not from Earth. I will turn off the ship's re-imaging shield and conserve energy. That will make it easier to lift off."

By the time he had finished starting the engine, several humans in identical blue uniforms had tumbled from the vehicles. They surrounded the alien's cruiser. When Baeznor flipped the switch deactivating the re-imaging shield, the humans began shouting and waving. A few even gesticulated with black curved pipes they held in their hands.

"Look! They came to say goodbye!" Zyphira exclaimed, waving her tentacles in glee.

The small ship rumbled and hovered for a few moments. Baeznor and Zyphira observed the humans one last time, reluctant to leave. *The humans really knew how to party!* Lights from inside the ship illuminated the occupants of the cruiser.

The humans gawked at the visitors. Some dropped their arms and froze; others waved more enthusiastically.

Zyphira and Baeznor peered out the window at the humans.

One human writhed with extreme excitement. His limbs shook spastically. Baeznor looked away from the commotion in front of him for a moment to input the return coordinates. The teens heard a barely audible crack originating from the group surrounding their ship. Then a brilliant fireball lit up the viewport.

The aliens observed the humans scurry about in celebration.

"The human fireworks are impressive! My progenitor did not tell me that the humans concluded their parties in this manner. I will need to inform him of this," Baeznor said.

"They were so nice and welcoming," Zyphira gushed. "And to send us off with such style! We will have to come back sometime."

Baeznor settled back into his seat, suckers pulsing with pleasure. *Yes, we will have to come back.*

The Bolide Railroad

By Natashja Maccormick

My eyes fluttered open to the high-pitched sound of a train whistle. My vision cleared up to see a dark blue ceiling above me. I was lying on a cold floor inside a train car. I pushed myself up off my back. A sting of pain surged through my head, causing me to hiss and grab one side of my head with a handcuffed hand. "Handcuffs?" I murmured. Then I remembered where I was before falling asleep.

"Neptune, hang on!" I screamed in response as my fingers slipped from the beam. I flew past my father's bloodied face into the machine's entryway, the machine that had suddenly malfunctioned. It began to tremble, then it convulsed and beeped, and the alarms wailed and wailed like an infant. Then it sucked the room into it, taking everything on the left side to another set of coordinates in the universe. I sat up against the wall, facing a set of bars blocking another car. Inside the car was someone chained to a silver throne. They wore all-black clothing up to their chin and had messy, almost neon-pink hair. The being raised his head and stared at me with yellow feline-esque eyes. They were oval-shaped and seemed to glow in nearby stars' light. His mouth had long, bumpy scars that ran up the sides of his face on either side.

A few moments after he woke up, a high-pitched beeping noise began and the lights in his room rapidly flickered on and off. A swooshing noise ended the beeping. I heard heavy boots walking through the train car. A short aqua-pink-haired boy in silver militia attire stood in front of the pink-haired one with his arms crossed. He had pouty lips, human eyes (except purple and bright green), and antennae on his head. Just barely visible under his clothing were two greenish-blue cords that I assumed were supposed to be some sort of neck.

"Caelan Castor Conroy!" The general huffed. "I'm trying to relax a bit before throwing the both of you in jail. Stop being so darn anxious."

The pink-haired cattish inmate, now known as Caelan, scoffed. "You don't have to track my anxiety levels, General. I told you that's not how I escape." Caelan turned his head back to look at me. "Also, the new guy is awake."

Mr. General turned around and sighed, pressing a button on one of his medals. The wall separating us folded up and left us in one big train car. Caelan smirked, crossing his legs.

"Hey, what you in for?"

"He appeared in a home on Jolon. Your home planet, right?" The general interrupted before I could respond.

"Indeed, that is where my parents happened to abandon me." Caelan hissed. "But what was he doing? Stealing?"

"No. He showed up unconscious, without an ID. Taiwo wanted to see him."

Caelan stood up from the throne. He strolled over to me, holding something behind his back that made clicking noises with every step. "I told you to stop doing that!" The general whined, getting up and snatching a set of keys out of Caelan's hands.

"Not my fault you were walking too close to me." Caelan shrugged.

"Ahem." I interrupted their bickering.

"Yes, Mr. Jolonian?" Caelan squawked.

"Who is Taiwo? Where am I? What is Jolon? Wh—"

The general laughed. "Calm down, little one," he said, taking out a pink beer bottle and drinking from it.

"Pretty sure you still aren't drinking age." Caelan scolded the general and attempted to snatch the bottle out of his hands.

The general moved his hand holding the bottle away and gripped Caelan's wrist in the other. "I'm only two years off; I'm fourteen now. I'm not a baby or anything."

"Sure, Galilei."

"Don't use my first name! Rotten pirates like you should address me properly!" The general stood up and stuck his nose up in Caelan's face. He was noticeably shorter than Caelan.

"Fine. Sure! General Moongenik! Happy?"

"I would hate to interrupt your bickering again, but I really need your help." I sniffled, thinking of the situation I was in just a few hours ago.

General Moongenik sat back down, this time turning the chair around and sitting in it backward as Caelan sat against General Moongenik's chair. "Go on."

"I'm from a planet called Earth. How far is it from here?"

Caelan and Moongenik glanced at each other, a smile breaking out on both faces as they burst into giggling. "Listen here, Earthling," Moongenik wiped a tear from his eye, "Earth was destroyed eons ago. What are you on about?"

"He must've gotten beaten up pretty badly on Jolon!" Caelan guffawed, his pupils shrinking with each laugh.

I faltered. "Destroyed?" I whispered. "By what?"

"Earth and Emrik destroyed one another in the Great Battle of Saturn's belt. You are certainly not from Earth if you don't even—"

"But I am!" I tugged at the handcuffs, flinching as Caelan's cell rapidly beeped again. "It isn't destroyed! We have just figured out teleportation!"

"And what is your name, Earthling?"

"Neptune. Neptune Andromeda. I come from Canada on Earth. Can't you believe me?"

"Well." Moongenik took another swig from his drink. "That is an earthly name, isn't it?"

"But what about his clothes?" Caelan looked at my yellow and black fighter jacket up and down. "They're so Metanoian!"

"What are these places you talk about?" I cringed as the handcuffs dug deeper into my wrists. "What galaxy is this?"

Caelan sighed and held his face in his hands. "Taxes galaxy. Taiwo's creation. Man, you hit your head pretty bad."

"Taxes?"

"No. Taxes. Tak-zees. Did you lose your hearing along with your mind?"

I felt the handcuffs slip off my wrists. I looked at Caelan first, assuming he had some weird telekinesis that enabled him to take off his own handcuffs and those of others. But I found Moongenik looking back at me with a smile. Or what I thought was a smile. His smile was full of teeth, rows and rows of teeth lining every inch of gum in his mouth. Razor-sharp teeth lightly shaded dark blue.

"He may be telling the truth after all."

Caelan tilted his head. "How did you come to that conclusion?"

"I ran a quick biology test on him just now. It says he's one hundred percent human!"

"One hundred?!" Caelan's jaw dropped as he gawked at me. "I thought they were extinct! Woah, Taiwo has got see this guy..."

"Who is Taiwo!?" I screeched, finally standing up with my wobbly legs. "Is he your god or something?"

"Precisely." Moongenik pulled a rock out of his back pocket and held it up to his lips. "DeCarlo! Set a course for Taiwo's planet as soon as possible."

"I know who your parents are, but still, how do you have this much power?" Caelan asked Moongenik while picking at his fingernails.

"You two wackos are the only ones on this train right now. It isn't a big deal." The two of them continued to bicker back and forth. I zoned out, looking out of the small barred window at the top of my train car. The stars were all sorts of colors. In my galaxy, they're all blue. Is something wrong with this galaxy's stars? Or mine? And so began my journey to Taiwo's planet.

Moongenik left the cells to do "general stuff" as Caelan described it, leaving me and the cat-eared man alone. I ignored him, instead staring at the stars and planets whizzing by the train's window. I felt the floor sink next to me. I turned my head and came face to face, maybe three centimeters away from Caelan. I gasped, pushing myself to the side and flinching as a sting arose in my palm. "So, Neptune, what planet were you born on?"

"Earth."

Caelan pouted. "Right. Right. I don't know where I was born, prob-ably on Metanoia? Definitely not Jolon, though that is where I grew up—"

"Why are you telling me this?"

"Because I have nothing else to do. I already broke out of my cell, my cuffs, and ate dinner. I mean, what else is there to do on a jail train?"

"I don't know," I murmured, curling in on myself and hugging my knees close to my body. I knew he was trying to distract me, but it wasn't working. I was still scared and wanted to get off this train as soon as possible.

"So Neptune and Andromeda... what's your story?"

"My story?" I repeated, almost incredulously. I shook my head. "I don't know. I don't have a story."

"Oh, come on, everyone has a story," he said, looking at me with a mischievous glint in his eye. "What's yours?"

"I was born and now I'm here. Happy?" I sneered. "That's it. That's my story. Nothing special."

He laughed and said, "I'm sure there's more to it than that. I bet you have some pretty interesting experiences to share, you know, living on Earth and all."

"What about you? What's your story?"

"I was born." Caelan giggled. "And then left on Jolon as a baby I think I was raised as a community effort, and yet here I am on the jail train." Caelan wistfully smiled. "I don't think anyone knew my real name or who my family was. I've been running from the law ever since I was old enough to understand what it meant. I'm just trying to make it to the next planet and stay one step ahead."

I nodded. The two of us continued to converse about whatever came to mind, trying to keep ourselves awake during the long (Moongenik said it would take six eropts to reach Taiwo's planet, I'm still not sure how that would translate to Earth time) journey to Taiwo's planet.

Eventually, we fell asleep, lulled by the steady hum of the train's engine and the gentle rocking motion of the tracks. Or what I assumed were tracks. I hadn't seen the outside of the train, so I had no idea what we were riding on. I awoke to Moongenik's gruff voice telling us we had arrived at our destination. I sat up and rubbed my eyes, trying to adjust to the darkness of the void. I could barely make out the silhouette of Taiwo's glowing, white planet in the distance through the window. "Caelan, get up!" Moongenik yelled, tapping a long metal stick to Caelan's ankle.

Caelan's eyes flew open. Moongenik then pressed a button on the stick, and Caelan was electrocuted with a sudden jolt of electricity. He let out a piercing scream as sparks flew from his body, and his entire body shook from the shock.

"What was that?!" I asked, my voice shaking with fear.

Moongenik smirked and said, "It's a special tool I use. It's called an electro-prod and it's a great way to get lazy people out of their slumber quickly."

"I'm up!" Caelan croaked, his eyes dilated to bigger than the moon.

"See, it works," Moongenik said, a malicious glint in his eye.

We stepped onto Taiwo's planet. It was gray and glowing white, with an endless forest ahead of us. Two people dressed similarly to Moongenik (Yet not physically like him at all; unlike the other two, they were green-skinned, taller than the trees, and smelled strongly of pineapple) led us through the forest. They each had glaring lanterns strapped to their legs to lead the way. Soon enough, a castle came into sight, its towers stretching up into the stars above. There was a single tower in the middle that seemed to stretch up even further. I quickly realized that this was the source of the glowing white light and where we were headed. Between the forest and the castle, stood an electric blue pond simmering in white light. I expected a gray boat to arrive to take us across.

Moongenik stepped into the water, dragging Caelan and me after him. I winced as the water hit my legs and a heavy vibration spread through my body. I felt like I could hear it, as if it was trying to speak to me. My legs were drenched in water when we reached the castle doors. It slipped off and back into the pond when we reached the castle doors. Moongenik waved the two guards off and led us through the castle. It glowed silver everywhere, making it difficult to see the endless staircases we had to climb up. We eventually reached a large door with intricate carvings.

Moongenik opened it and stepped aside for us to enter. Inside was a grand hall with a long table in the center, surrounded by several chairs. At the end of the table sat a man with a set of antelope-esque horns on his head, wearing a gray-and-green robe. He had a long black veil over his face, but his blue eyes were deep enough to pierce through the veil. He was surrounded by a few... unusual beings. One of them was the most human-like being I had seen so far. This one had glittery dark hair, wore white and silver robes and kept a hand on the elder being's shoulders as we made our way down the table.

The young being bowed to us, to which I hesitantly bowed back. "My name is Orionne. This is my father, Taiwo. What brings you here?"

I gulped as Moongenik gave Taiwo a small bow. "This is the unidenti-fied being Taiwo wanted to see. The one from Jolon."

"I see." Orionne nodded, placing a hand over Taiwo's forehead and waking him up with a flash of white light. Taiwo gradually stood up on two thinly furred deer legs. He towered over us by several feet and wore shredded black clothing beneath his robe. Taiwo looked down at us, specifically at me, before turning to Moongenik. "Greetings, General Moongenik." His voice was hoarse and fleeting, as if it was the voice of a singing show bird in the late stages of its life.

Moongenik bowed his head. "Greetings, Taiwo. You wanted me to bring this being here?"

"Yes. Thank you, Moongenik." Taiwo leaned down close enough to breathe directly into my nostrils. He smelled like edelweiss with a hint of thick and old dust. His breath was freezing cold, colder than fresh snow in Antarctica and as brief as the present moment. "What galaxy do you come from?"

I gulped. "The Milkyway, uh- sir."

A crackling noise made its way through the veil. "I see. That's quite far from here. Whatever are you doing in Taxes?"

I glanced at Caelan, who looked just as pale and stiff as I did under the intimidating beast. "I got lost. My father built a teleportation machine, and it malfunctioned."

"Really?" Taiwo tilted his head to one side, the jewelry hanging off his horns clinking. "Which planet do you come from?"

"Earth, sir."

"Impossible." Taiwo hissed like a snake. "Earth was destroyed many centuries ago. I watched it."

I shook my head. "I don't understand... How could that be?"

Taiwo sat back down. He leaned back in his seat with his head up to the ceiling. "Perhaps you weren't teleported but sent through time."

"That's crazy," I muttered, faltering as my tone replayed in my head. I felt Caelan and Moongenik gasp beside me. "Time travel is impossible."

"It is impossible..." Taiwo paused. "In your time. But not in mine."

"Then!" I shook my head as fast as I could. I was trying to regain focus, trying desperately to steady my thumping heart. "How did I end up on Jolon?!"

"The universe is always moving. Where it is heading, not even I know."

A pounding pain shot through my head as I tried to comprehend what I was hearing. I was trying to make sense of the situation, but my mind was running in circles. I felt like I had stepped into a dream, and I desperately wanted to wake up. "How do I return home?"

"You may never return home," Taiwo said, his voice heavy with sadness. His words felt like a punch in the gut, and I felt my heart sink. I couldn't be with my father to release his groundbreaking invention to the world, I couldn't take care of my younger brother anymore, I wouldn't get to see him go to college or even finish high school, I could never get married, I could never—"But." I perked up. "There is one way. That is why I said it wasn't impossible in our time."

Taiwo looked to Moongenik. "General Moongenik?"

"Yes?"

"Will you complete something for me?"

"Of course!" Moongenik bowed. "Any time! Just tell me what we have to do!"

"You must take Neptune to Zasth. There, you must reach the core and extract some of its essence." Taiwo paused and clutched the side of his head with a clawed hand. "Then bring the essence back to me, and I will use it to send Neptune back."

"Got it! Let's go!" Moongenik cheered, practically flying around the room with excitement bursting out of his small figure.

"Are you gonna drop me off on Atuvn first?"

"Pfft." Moongenik wrapped an arm around Caelan's shoulders (What he could reach of them anyway.) "No, silly. You're coming along!"

"What?! I don't want to—"

Caelan's whining was halted by a slap across the face from Moongenik. "It is the order of Taiwo, you fool! You are coming whether you want to or not!" Moongenik told us this trip would take ten eropts. Five eropts in, we stopped on a planet known as Parsphaera, or as Caelan called it, "The party planet," equipped with places to drink this galaxy's only form of alcohol, places beings of all shapes, sizes, and matters could stay for however many eropts they needed to and countless dark alleyways that Moongenik told me to avoid at all costs. The hotel we stayed in was glittery and white, filled with beings with intimidating auras and harsh stares, from what I could only assume were their eyes.

"But Moongenik told us to stay put."

"So?" Caelan wiggled an eyebrow. "Don't you want to see more of the universe while you have the chance?"

I bit my bottom lip. "What do you have in mind?"

Clubbing in the Taxes Galaxy was very similar to clubbing I had briefly seen on television. Colorful flashing lights, loud music, and drinks. Caelan led me through a crowd of beings squished together inside of a pit inside of another pit inside of a skyscraper-esque building. Every being held the same thin, glistening pink bottles in their hands, filled with an invisible liquid. The drink tasted like Earth's air. Empty and clear. But Caelan enjoyed it. With each sip, his pupils shrank further into their golden sea.

The cattish man became more hyper as the ... whatever they called it on Parsphaera continued on. Eventually, I was spun around the dance floor without my legs touching the ground. He laughed and sang along with the music, and I could feel the energy of the entire room around us. Eventually, the music ended, and I staggered off the dance floor with a spacey Caelan in tow, exhausted but grinning from ear to ear.

Caelan explained that the music would return in a few minutes. Some beings couldn't handle high volumes for long periods of time. This started an entire historical movement in the galaxy that ended with several changes to current noise laws. A beat of silence passed between us. I reached out toward the scar lining Caelan's face, gently running my fingers along each bump. "How did you get these?" Caelan's entire being turned red. A deep human-blood-cardinal-feather-cherry-skin red. His pupils sank into their sockets more than I thought was possible, and he couldn't push any words out of his clenched jaw.

"You—" Caelan finally spoke in a jarring, cough-like tone. "You can see them?"

"See what?"

"My scars... You can see my scars?"

"Yes." I frowned. "Why?"

"Never mind. Let's head back before Moongenik finds out we're gone." A few Earth hours later, we took off into the dead of space toward Zasth. Or as Moongenik called it, the blue planet of Taxes. Zasth was glowing sky blue. Specks of gray spread across the vast blueness but were mostly hidden by the blue's blinding shimmer.

We landed on a thin piece of gray sand, where beings the size of otters and the shapes of crabs greeted us, discussing something with Moongenik in another language before we took off on a small boat. The ocean was sky blue and opaque, almost milk-like in texture and shimmering against the violet sun. "Can you breathe underwater?" Moongenik snapped me out of my thoughts and back into the field of cotton candy blue.

"No. Why? Aren't we—"

"Just digging to the bottom. That's right. I had forgotten what we came to Zasth to do in the first place."

"Erm. How far down does the water go?"

"Only about a hundred rintiks."

Caelan snickered. "Only? He can't breathe underwater!"

"Then he can stay on the boat! I don't believe that you ever think about things, Conroy!" Moongenik pressed a button on his suit, and up came a glass sphere over his head and around his antennae. Caelan, on the other hand dived right into the water, disappearing in an instant. I stared at the mauve rays of light above me. The water below me began to tremble and ripples spread as far as I could see. Behind me, a wave towered over the ripples and rushed toward our small boat.

I leaned over the side of the boat and yelled for Moongenik. The wave crashed over the boat, knocking me off my feet and plunging me into the freezing water. I sank down into the depths of the ocean, absorbing the cold water surrounding me. I frantically searched for something to grab onto. However, the raging waves kept me descending until my head grew so light that I thought it would float back up without the rest of my body.

Eventually, I felt a hand grab my wrist and pull me up to the surface. I was thrown back onto the boat and immediately felt hands running over my neck and chest. I heard muffled voices discussing something above me, but I had no way of knowing who it was due to the water dying my vision sky blue. I shivered, feeling a chill run through my body as I lay there. I tried to speak, but all that came out was a faint whisper.

My vision cleared up, and I came face to face with Caelan. However, he had gills lining his body from his collarbone up to his nose. His eyes were deep blue, and for once, he had a glimmer of intelligence. "Like the new look?"

I nodded, swallowing the last remnant of sugary seawater in my mouth. "What was that?"

"I have the feeling that the water here isn't quite the same as your Earth water."

Moongenik chimed in. "Doesn't it eat beings?" I glanced nervously around, wondering what else lurked beneath the aquamarine depths. Moongenik smiled, the corners of his eyes crinkling. "It's alright, we can head back now. We successfully extracted some of Zasth's essence!"

All of a sudden, Caelan tugged my head toward him. He stared me straight in the eyes as the blue faded from his own and returned to their original yellow. "Can you still see them?"

"Your scars?"

"My scars."

I nodded. Caelan's scars were more obvious than they were on Parsphaera, sticking out of his face as if reaching for me.

Moongenik shrieked, covering his mouth with his armored hands. "He can see your scars! How—"

Caelan shushed Moongenik and gave him a slight nod. "Don't worry about it. I have eighteen lives left, anyway." We boarded the train and began our ten eropt trip back to Taiwo's planet. Caelan and I sat side-by-side, chatting about what would come next.

He was worried about seeing Taiwo again. He was worried that he would suddenly recognize him as a pirate and drain the eighteen lives he had left from his body. Eventually, we stopped again at Parsphaera. This time, Caelan didn't want to leave our room. Instead, he stared at me, seemingly convinced he was being sneaky with his quick turns away and awkward glances. I asked him what was going on, but he refused to answer. He said he'd tell me soon if he needed to and asked once more if I could still see his scars.

We arrived at Taiwo's castle. I noticed Caelan growing more jumpy and pale as we ascended each staircase as if we were walking toward the guillotine that would execute him for his crimes. Oronne stood at the end of the table with his father. His expression was full of resentment, his nails digging deep into Taiwo's bloody shoulders while he watched us walk down the hall.

"Taiwo, my Lord..." Moongenik bowed at Taiwo's feet. "We have brought you the essence of Zasth so that Neptune may return home."

"Brilliant." Taiwo stood up, grabbing the jar of Zasth essence from Moongenik's hand. Then he grabbed the back of my jacket and lifted me up as he stood. I gulped, glancing at the ground, which felt thousands of feet below me. My heart raced as I looked up at Taiwo with wide eyes. His head was bigger than my body, the veil covering his face long gone as I looked into his dizzying eyes, feeling like they were the portals that would send me back home, as if I would fall into them and never come out or they would wrap around my body and squish me into oblivion. I was lowered to face Taiwo's mouth. He grinned, revealing rows and rows of twisted teeth with sharp edges.

"I miss the energy you earthlings gave off. Too bad your planet was destroyed before I reached full power." My heart plummeted to the ground as Taiwo's words graced my ears. I forced myself to look away, but his words kept ringing in my ears. I had no way of knowing how much truth was in his words or what had happened to the planet I called home. All I could do was hang there and hope that it wasn't true, hope that this galaxy's god had a dark sense of humor and that I'd be sent home any second now.

Taiwo leaned back and opened his mouth. His teeth began to spin around in silence as his tongue danced around them, grazing each tooth and drawing Taiwo's orange blood from its body. I watched in horror as his teeth spun faster and faster, and he cackled. His laughter echoed through the dining hall, and I knew that I was doomed. I closed my eyes and accepted my fate. I figured Caelan and Moongenik were either too loyal or too weak to save me from Taiwo's stomach. As my legs dangled over Taiwo's mouth, my shirt collar pressed against my throat, causing my eyes to pop open. The beast lowered me closer and closer to his drilled, pyramid-shaped teeth.

They spun around like blender blades, ready to shred my energy to bits while poor little Moongenik and Caelan watched. I struggled against the hand holding my jacket, trying to swing away from the jaws of Taiwo. A pair of arms wrapped around my waist and I hurtled toward the ground. Above me, I caught a glimpse of my savior, Caelan, being tugged toward Taiwo's mouth by some invisible force and quickly disappearing behind his jaw. I screamed his name, the wind tearing at my voice and carrying it away. My heart raced, pounding in my chest as I fell. I could feel the ground rushing up to meet me.

Moongenik yelled in the distance, rushing toward where I would land as if he could break my fall. His eyes were wide with fear as he sprinted toward me. But it was too late. I felt the ground hard against my back and a grinding sting shot up my spine. I saw a bright light before everything became dark. I heard Moongenik's distant voice calling my name, and then nothing.

And then everything as the world bloomed back around me. I made eye contact with Orionne, whose eyes had exploded into two cities of stars and whose skin had wrinkled to the point of making him resemble an elderly human being. He held me from below, whispering a mantra while my spine trembled and my blood splattered across the floor, drained itself back into my body. "I can send you back. You must hurry.' Orionne spoke, his hands placing my weakened figure down.

I held up a hand and cleared my throat as Taiwo returned to his senses and searched for me. "What about Caelan?"

"He'll reappear any moment now!" Moongenik yelled over Taiwo's screams. "But I don't believe that you have enough time!" I pushed myself off the ground, struggling to stay up on my arms as the ground trembled and swayed beneath us.

"Won't Taiwo hurt him after this?"

"He will be alright," Moongenik assured me. "You must trust me and go!" As if conjured from thin air, Caelan appeared and made a vomiting motion with his mouth.

"That was so gross!" He cried. "Neptune! Can you still see my scars?"

Orionne looked between us and grabbed Caelan by the arm, tugging him to me and attaching his hand to my wrist before smashing open the jar of Zasth essence and opening his hands until they stretched far enough to cover my view of the world around me.

I felt Caelan's grip on my wrist tighten as we flew through the stars. I felt the warmth of the Zasth essence spread through my body, and as it did, I noticed the stars around us brighten. Then, just as quickly as it had started, the moment was over, and we were back on solid ground.

My father rushed in through the laboratory door, his eyes widening to the size of the moon as they caught sight of me. He rushed over and hugged me, tears streaming down his face. "Oh Neptune! I thought I lost you... Are you hurt? Did anything happen? How much time passed for you? Did—"

I looked at Caelan and beamed, feeling the warmth of the Zasth essence leaving me. My father turned to Caelan and jumped. "What is that?"

"That's Caelan." I gently pushed myself away from my father. "He helped me get back, and he needed some help in return." I took a deep breath of real Earth air, reveling in the feeling of stability that came with it. "I can only hope Moongenik is safe, too."

Caelan rested a hand on my shoulder. "He has his ways. I wouldn't worry about him too much." He paused. "Are my scars still there?" Where Caelan's scars once were, they remained as only light white lines, completely invisible to beings who didn't know they were there in the first place. I shook my head.

"Can you tell me what they mean now?"
Caelan chuckled. "Nah. You'll figure it out, Andromeda."

The Forbidden Wastes

By Kay Hanifen

Most sentient species assert that the planet they live on is special. It's different from all the other worlds that support life, and I'm not going to say it isn't beautiful or vital to the survival of that species. But Keyae truly is different from other worlds. Keyae is intelligent. If you listen close enough, it tells you its will and shows you how to help not only your own species, but the other highly intelligent species that call this world home.

For as long as anyone can remember, the Yuna have sailed through the sky, the Kestra have traversed the earth, and the Efra have swum in the oceans. Every town and village appoints a Listener from each of the species that lives there to advocate for Keyae and to tell the town its will.

I am the Yuna Listener for my town. Like the rest of my species, my ears are so sensitive that I can pick up even the softest whisper from Keyae even while flying through the air. It comforts me to hear its voice, to know I'm fulfilling its will alongside my fellow Listeners. I know they feel it too. The connection is indescribable—like you're nothing but a cell in a massive living organism, but despite your insignificance, you know you serve a function. You have a duty to keep the body healthy, not just for yourself, but for everything else within it.

Lately, though, something about Keyae feels unbalanced. My fellow

Listeners, Oprine the Kestra and Mlio the Efra, have noticed as well. I think it's because of the newest arrival on our planet. A small group of beings calling themselves humans have made their home on this world, but they have not yet appointed a Listener to better understand what the planet wishes for them to do.

Humans are a strange breed. Anatomically, they perhaps most resemble my species, the Yuna. They are bipedal and closer in height, but they have no skin connecting hands to feet, allowing them to fly. Their ears are much smaller, and they have no fur to keep them warm, instead wearing a false covering that they remove and change depending on the weather. In that way, they're similar to the Kestra, but that is where it mostly ends. Kestra are quadrupedal, their hide is much tougher, and their trunks act as a third hand to hold and manipulate the world around them.

The species the humans least resemble is the Efra. Because the Efra are an aquatic species, they must wear water tanks to breathe. Their appendages are mostly tentacles with suction cups to make it easier to hold things. For a while, our society on land has struggled to accommodate them just as they've struggled to accommodate us in the water, but we've managed to make it work.

The humans have mostly kept to themselves, only participating in our society when invited. Well, all except one: Polly, who visits us at our temple almost every day. She told me she's a young adult of her species and is curious about how we coexist with an intelligent planet. It's nice to see that she's interested in our society. It gives me hope that humans will be able to fully integrate into our world someday.

"Tria," she said one morning as she wrote in a notebook that never seemed to leave her hands, "How do you listen to your planet? What does it look like?"

"It might be easier if I show you," I replied, getting to my feet and leading her deeper into the temple, down to the basement, and then through the sacred door carved with images of important events on our world. It let out into a cave system illuminated by mushrooms, algae, and luminescent rock. My preferred spot was further back, so that the noise of the temple above wouldn't be a distraction.

Her eyes were wide with wonder as I sat her down in a quiet, dark alcove. I removed my shoes and pressed my bare hands and feet to the earth floor below. Inhaling and exhaling, my body relaxed as the peace of Keyae spread through me. Polly was still standing, holding herself as though unsure if she should join. I smiled and beckoned her to sit beside me.

"Are-are you sure? I don't want to offend the planet or your culture by doing it wrong or even doing it at all if I'm not supposed to."

I tilted my head. "Is that why the humans are afraid to join us?"

She let out a strange, barking sound. I've come to learn that this is a laugh, something done either because a human finds a situation humorous or because they find it awkward and want to defuse the tension. "On our world, we kind of have a history of doing more harm than good when dealing with outside cultures, so we're trying to keep our distance and let you come to us."

"Except you," I said, nodding to the notebook in her hand.

Looking down at it, she said, "Just because we don't want to barge into your culture and take it over, it doesn't mean we don't want to learn about you. They call me an ambassador, which is sort of like a Listener, except I learn about what the intelligent species on a planet want instead of what the planet itself wants."

Suddenly understanding everything, I nodded and patted for her to sit beside me. "I thought it was odd that the humans had not yet appointed a Listener for your village, but it looks like you all did in your own way. Come here. If your kind plan on staying, you must learn how to connect with Keyae."

Grinning widely—an expression I've learned is a sign of happiness rather than aggression—she took off her shoes and sa- beside me. "Now, what do we do?"

I took a slow, deep breath in and out. "Clear your mind and listen to every little sound. Feel the earth beneath you and let yourself become one with Keyae." We sat in silence. The first attempt at Listening can be difficult, so while she waited, I slipped into a more receptive state.

Eyes closed, I found myself in the Forbidden Wastes. Nothing grew here. Not since our planet's first and only war where the weapons and the pain scarred Keyae itself. The memories of that terrible battle live there, but memories for a planet are a living thing. The heat from the explosions still sear skin and the air still smells of mud and decay. We dare not venture there, both out of respect for Keyae's pain, and for our own safety.

But now I stood among the abandoned bones of the fallen. Why would it show me this terrible place?

And then I saw it. Like a shooting star, a vessel streaked across the sky and crash-landed in the fields of pain. A human crawled out of the vessel before turning and helping another wounded soul escape. More soon pulled themselves free while dragging out as much of the ship as they could. Then, the ship caught fire, exploding like the bombs of old and knocking several of them back.

A scream.

It shook me out of my vision, the terror and grief far too real to be a message from Keyae. "Polly!" I exclaimed, grabbing her hands. "Polly, listen to me. You're safe."

"But they aren't," she said, pulling away and staggering to her feet. "Did you see it, too? Do you know where they might've crashed?"

Following her, I said, "Yes, but—"

"But nothing. I have to help them. Where are they?"

I snatched her wrist, forcing her to stop and turn to me. "Slow down. No one goes into the Forbidden Wastes. It's too dangerous. I'm sorry, but they are already dead."

"If that was true, why would Keyae show me the crash? You told me to listen to its will, and I think it wants me to save them."

"What's going on here?" Oprine, the Kestra Listener, asked as they emerged from the shadows. Their massive body barely fit in the cave, but they somehow managed.

Mlio clung to their trunk, clearly enjoying the ride as they swung em back and forth. The two had always been close, something that I tried not to let myself feel jealous of. They had been raised in the temple, essentially chosen from birth to be Listeners. I arrived much later. The Yona before me died as a child, and I was the second choice. At the time, I was seen as the replacement. The interloper. And they resented me.

But that was years ago. I may not be as close to them as they are to each other, but we get along well enough.

Polly tried to push past them, but Mlio held out a tentacle to stop her. "Where are you going, friend?"

I explained the vision and her desire to mount a rescue mission. Mlio shook aer head. "Polly, I'm terribly sorry, but like Tria said, they're already dead. Nothing lives in the Forbidden Wastes. Not for long anyway."

"What happened there?" she asked, her arms crossed and eyes glancing toward the door as though she was planning to make a run for the exit.

"We have only ever fought one war between the species," Oprine said, lowering herself down to sit. "It was early in our history, and over something foolish like who has domain over what. Tensions rose until, like a pustule, it had to burst and unleashed its infection upon the rest of the world."

"But when it came time for battle, Keyae was horrified by the slaughter," Mlio said, jumping in, "It loves everything that lives on it in the same way a mother loves a child. It didn't want its children to squabble out of greed and petty, wounded pride."

"The battlefield left a scar on the very earth itself," I said. "Keyae cannot seem to heal from the suffering of that day, and those that try to commune with it to heal the wounds experience nothing but pain and suffering for the rest of their short, miserable lives."

Polly shook her head. "You don't understand. My wife was on that ship. She's a doctor, and it's full of medical supplies and other necessities for survival, not just for me but for my community. I'm going no matter what."

"I'll go with you," I said, surprising myself. Over the past few weeks, I'd come to see Polly as a friend, and I didn't want to see her get hurt, even if it meant traveling to the Forbidden Wastes.

Her eyes widened in surprise, and she said, "Oh, no, Tria. I wouldn't ask that of you."

"Which is why I'm offering," I replied.

Oprine slowly got to their feet. "I'm coming too. You'll need someone strong enough to carry the wounded and the medical supplies."

"And I can treat the injured," Mlio said. "I'm something of a doctor myself. When I'm not Listening, I mean." The Efra are known for their technological talents and ability to heal others, but Mlio is brilliant even among their most revered scientists. In addition to aer duties, Mlio had set bones, performed surgery, and even delivered a Kestra baby. Ae spent aer free time in aer bedroom tinkering away at one device or another. Ae was perhaps the most qualified to administer any necessary first aid.

Her eyes welled with water, which then streamed down her face. We all exchanged uncomfortable glances. Mlio spoke first, asking, "Polly, why are you leaking?"

She barked a wet laugh that didn't have any of the mirth I'd come to associate with her. "I'm not leaking. I'm crying. Because I'm scared that I'll be too late or end up hurting you or finding my wife's body. And I'm crying because I'm touched that I have friends who will put themselves in danger for me."

Oprine squinted at her, the twitching of their ears betraying their befuddlement. "And why do these strong feelings make your eyes leak?"

She shrugged, wiping the moisture away. "I actually don't know."

We all exchanged glances. Human biology was strange. Finally, Mlio said, "We should get ready. The journey will be dangerous, and we need to leave as soon as possible if we want to find them alive."

We agreed to meet at the temple gates in an hour with all our necessities.

Once the supplies were loaded and Oprine was strapped to the carriage, they were to drag into the Forbidden wastes, we set off without telling anyone else at the temple. They almost certainly would have stopped us, but I had a feeling that Keyae didn't want us to be stopped.

Polly was silently writing in her notebook while Mlio adjusted the settings on aer water tank to ensure that aer gills would be properly oxygenated throughout the journey. I didn't like this silence. Usually, Polly was peppering me with a million questions about Keyae and our society, but she had withdrawn, her tree bark brown skin now ashen. I missed her lively conversation and endless curiosity.

We were getting close, so I got to my feet and said, "I'm going to scout ahead so Oprine knows where to go."

Polly gave a wan smile. "Thank you, Tria. I owe you."

"We're friends," I said, opening the window to take flight. "You owe me nothing." I leaped out of the carriage and into the air, spreading my wings and gliding on an updraft. I've always loved the infinite openness of the sky. I loved the chill of the wind as it carried me higher and higher, my soul growing giddy with the lack of oxygen combined with the total freedom of flight.

I'd never voice it out loud, but a part of me believes that we Yona are the most blessed by Keyae. We may not be incredibly strong like the Kestra or technologically advanced like the Efra, but we were the only ones that are capable of venturing to all domains. We could walk on land, swim in water, and sail high above the clouds.

After I became a Listener, though, I had fewer and fewer opportunities to fly, to feel the wind coursing all around me and experience the meditative pumping of my wings. This flight was the first I'd taken in weeks, if not months, and I wished that it was under better circumstances.

The transition from the rest of Keyae to the Forbidden Wastes is sudden and jarring. It used to be farmland before it was the site of a battle, but despite the regular rainfall, nothing grew there now. It was all brown earth, occasionally broken up by craters and the metal shells of long abandoned vehicles. The elements had barely touched these behemoth monuments to the death and destruction that occurred here. From above, I could see the occasional white bone or Kestra tusk.

The story I learned from my history teacher was that no one really knows what this war was about. It could have been over resources or Keyae's will or simply because one species believed itself superior to the other. The why doesn't matter. It's been lost to history. What does matter is that it hurt Keyae and how the planet reacted to the pain of its three precious species fighting among themselves. Every tread from the vehicle shells below me, every crater pockmarking the ground, left a scar upon this world. Our planet lashed out with a profound grief, causing all the rivers, oceans, and lakes to flood, and ruining the harvest. During those dark times, it wasn't just the whispered guidance of the planet in the way we experience Keyae now. Keyae screamed with every explosion, every senseless death. No earplugs could reduce the sound, and it left many Yona with permanent hearing damage.

Many tried to leave the battlefield, but they had no hope of deserting. The panic had scattered the soldiers, leading to a worse slaughter as we reverted to our animal desires to escape the pain. And then an earthquake split the battlefield down the middle, the planetary equivalent to a time-out chair. Everything stopped at once. All sides of the conflict decided that this was a warning cry, and the next one would be far deadlier than a couple pieces of broken glass and some cases of tinnitus.

So, in their wisdom, the sides made peace. They returned any prisoners of war and found a way to get along. Over the centuries, we've grown quite talented at collaboration. If we didn't, then Keyae would likely punish us for another meaningless war.

Nothing grew in the Forbidden Wastes, and nothing that ventured into it came out alive. It was just miles and miles of dirt and mud, forever scarred by the memories of that day. It is said that anyone who ventures within goes insane from all the pain and terror. At least, that's how the story goes. I've heard it a thousand times ever since I was a child, and the details always seemed to be changing and warping to best suit the needs of the storyteller. I've heard stories using it as a backdrop warning against stranger danger or a promise for a better life in exchange for the soul of the person they love. Most often of all, though, it explains to us why there is no war on Keyae and frightens us away from the idea of trying to start one.

Finally, I spotted the remains of a small spacecraft just a short distance away. It glinted in the light of the late afternoon. Six humans were in the process of cataloging what they could salvage and tending to the wounded. There were some injuries, but there did not seem to be anything dire. Checking the position of the sun to estimate how much time we had, I turned and began the short flight to Oprine and the rest of this makeshift rescue mission.

As I flew, I had the distinct feeling of being watched from below. It felt as though the entirety of the Forbidden Wastes was judging me and finding me lacking as I returned to my friends.

Oprine had made it to the borders by the time I returned, their eyes wide and roving as though waiting for a predator to strike. I landed on the back of their head, right between their massive ears, and said, "The ship is about a klar east. If we don't stop, we should be able to make it there within an hour."

"Tria?" Polly asked, poking her head out of the carriage. "Did you find the ship? How badly were they all hurt?"

"Some minor injuries, but nothing seemed life-threatening," I reported.

Her shoulders relaxed as a smile spread across her face. "Thank you."

I climbed in through the window and I reported my findings to Mlio, who began prepping the medical supplies. I think we all felt the transition from the rest of the world to the Forbidden Wastes. From the sky, it's unsettling to feel, but now that I was indirectly connected to the earth, it hit me in a rush.

Mlio and Polly must have felt it, too, because they both shivered. Polly's face had gone gray, while Mlio's skin color changed to reflect the chair behind em. "Wow," Polly said, "You weren't kidding. This place is… I don't know. It feels bad. Like when I stayed at a haunted house on Earth. Is Oprine okay?"

"I'll go check on them," I said, climbing out the window. Taking flight, I fluttered in front of them. "How are you doing?"

"They're still here," Oprine muttered. "Keyae trapped them. This is now the land of the dead."

Landing on the top of their head, I rubbed their ears the way they liked it. "Hey, it's okay. We're all here, and we'll all get out together."

Their trunk reached back and grabbed me by the waist, pulling me down to meet their eyes. "You're not touching the ground. You cannot feel Keyae the way I can. You can't see what I see."

With that, they threw me to the ground. I sank into the mud, too stunned to do anything but listen to the sucking sounds Oprine made with every step. After I was orphaned as a child, I had a recurring nightmare of being trapped in my family home as it burned. In the waking world, I escaped, but in this dream, I was frozen, paralyzed as my parents' fur caught fire while they screamed and begged for my help. But I could only stand there and watch them burn.

Touching the earth and hearing Keyae's scream mingled with the screams of the long-dead battlefield reminded me of those terrible dreams where I never escaped the worst moments of my life. I felt the fire in my face, watched my body be torn apart by bullets and knives and explosions, and smelled the odor of blood, exhaust, and excrement on the battlefield. It was as though I was experiencing the suffering of every wounded and dying soul in the battle at once. Just like when I was a child, I was helpless against the battery of memories like driving rain in a hurricane.

As a child, I woke up in the morning to the knowledge that I was safe and unhurt. The wounds upon my body and soul became nothing more than scar tissue. It was still fresh for Keyae, even after all these centuries. The pain and the grief were a raw wound that the planet picked at, keeping it from scabbing over and eventually healing.

For most of my life, Listening to Keyae brought me peace. My time below ground felt a lot like my parents' embraces. Though it always spoke to me, I rarely spoke to it. Now, I pushed my own feelings down into the earth, praying that Keyae would hear what I had to say. *The war is over. We have healed, and you no longer have to suffer.*

I heard a scream from up ahead and then a crash. Struggling to my feet, I shook off the mud and flew in the direction where Oprine was headed. The sun was going down, the sky erupting in brilliant reds, pinks, and purples.

Soon, the carriage came into view, but Oprine was long gone. They must have ripped it off before fleeing further into the wastes. Polly was outside, clearly assessing the damage. Mlio had either fled or was still inside gathering medical supplies.

Seeing me, Polly waved her arms, beckoning me down. Though I'd managed to keep my sanity when I connected with the earth, I didn't want to experience it again, so I landed on top of the broken carriage.

"Are you okay? What happened?" she asked, her eyes skimming over my body for any signs of injury.

"I could ask you the same thing," I replied. "Is Mlio still with you?"

"In here," a faint voice called from the inside.

"Don't come out. It's the earth itself that's causing this."

"Why isn't it affecting me?" Polly asked. She glanced down at her muddy clothing and then back up to where I sat. "It feels wrong here, but Oprine just went crazy. It was like they wanted us to suffer as much as they were suffering."

"Perhaps you're less attuned to Keyae and its will," Mlio suggested. "You aren't from around here, after all." I shot em a glare, but aer face was diplomatically blank.

"Mlio," I began, but Polly shook her head.

"No, that makes sense. You three spent your lives listening to Keyae, but I've only ever done it once." The human buried her face in her hands. "This is my fault. I shouldn't have dragged you out here."

Taking flight once more, I fluttered down to her side and squeezed her shoulder. Touching the ground still made my heart pound, but like the nightmares, I set it aside to focus on her. "We chose to help you find them. You couldn't have known what would happen."

"So, what do we do now?" Polly asked, glancing in the direction of the crashed spaceship that had carried her people. She looked torn between continuing the rescue or going after Oprine.

And if I was being honest, I felt conflicted. The humans were injured, and I wasn't sure how long they could wait before rescue, but Oprine was out there, and they were terrified and in pain.

"We go to whoever's closer," Mlio suggested.

That was as good a plan as any, so pumping my wings, I took off and circled the former battlefield. I spotted Oprine first, and then the human camp. They were barreling toward the stranded people, charging like an animal. Any minute now, they were going to be trampled by my friend. Swooping back down, I exclaimed, "Both of you get on. We have to hurry."

"Can you carry both of us?" Polly asked.

"Oprine is about to stampede the crash site, so I have to." While the Yona are not especially strong, we are capable of carrying twice our body weight as we fly. Polly and Mlio both got on my back, and I began pumping as hard as my wings would allow as I took to the air. Every muscle burned, but I kept on pushing, necessity and adrenaline fueling my flight. In minutes, we overtook Oprine, and then we were at the crash site.

"Janai!" Polly shouted, leaping off my back.

A dark-skinned woman picked up her head, her eyes wide with surprise. "Polly? What are you doing here? I—mmph!" Whatever she was about to say was drowned out by her wife throwing her arms around her shoulders and pulling her into a tight hug.

"I'm so glad you're safe!"

"But not for long," Mlio said, aer tentacles still suctioned to my back. "One of our friends has been driven mad by this place, and they're baring down on us as we speak."

"Will anyone be unable to walk out of here?" I asked.

"We'll live," Janai replied, her arms still wrapped snugly around Polly's waist.

Peeling Mlio off my back, I handed em to Polly. "Mlio, you can guide them out of here. I'll try to get through to Oprine."

"But—" ae and Polly protested in unison.

"Mlio, you can't touch the ground, and Polly, you're needed with your family. I'll be okay." With that, I took off once more, not even sparing a glance behind me, and praying to Keyae for their safety.

I found Oprine nearby. They were bucking, rearing, and swiping with their trunk as though they were being attacked. They trumpeted so loudly that it hurt my sensitive ears, and I let out a screech of my own, hoping the noise would get their attention. No luck. "Oprine!" I yelled, flittering near their sensitive ear. "Oprine, there's nothing there."

They swatted at me, their trunk hitting me square in the chest and knocking me to the ground.

And suddenly, I wasn't in a desolate, muddy field with Oprine. I was in the middle of a battle again, the mortar shells exploding around me and drowning out the screams of the wounded and the dying. I covered my ears and took shelter behind one of the Efra's amphibious vehicles. My heart pounded, lungs burning like I'd inhaled a wildfire's weight in smoke.

Oprine fought nearby, their trunk swiping Yona out of the sky midair and feet crushing Efra below. Their body was caked in blood and earth. Soldiers began swarming on all sides, shooting them or attempting to force a spear through their thick hide.

"Oprine," I called out, finally making myself visible. "Oprine, listen to me. This is only a memory. You aren't really here, and nothing is trying to kill you."

Trumpeting, they charged. I leaped up and grabbed them by the ears. Using it as leverage, I pulled myself up to wrap myself around the back of their neck, the closest we could get to a hug. "You're safe. The war is long over. We've all healed and have lived for centuries in peace. Oprine—Keyae—please hear me. This is nothing but a nightmare."

"Oprine! Tria!" Polly called from a distance. And then she was there with Mlio wrapped around her.

Oprine hesitated, their breath coming out in loud pants. "What...?"

Mlio leaped off Polly's shoulders and scurried up Oprine's back. "Whatever you're doing, it's working," ae said, reaching down to help Polly up.

"Keyae, I know it hurts, but it's just a memory," I said. "Look, Yona, Kestra, and Efra all in one place. And someone new. A human from the stars. We're all living together in peace. More than that. We're family. So please, let the wounds heal and free Oprine from your memories."

The sound of mortar and sight of dead bodies slowly vanished. It was replaced by the barren earth with just me, Oprine, Polly, and Mlio sitting in silence. Oprine fell to their front knees, gasping for breath. "Oh, Keyae," she whispered.

The pain, grief, and terror weren't fully gone, but it felt as though a heavy weight had been lifted from the land. We quickly found the humans, and though we lacked a carriage, we could give the more seriously injured a ride. The rest of us walked to the human encampment. Everyone who saw us leaving the Forbidden Wastes watched with their jaws hanging open, and they welcomed us back with open arms.

When we returned the next day for the humans' abandoned medical supplies, grass had begun to grow once more in the Forbidden Wastes for the first time in centuries.

Techno-Babble

By Megan Mackie

"**W**ait, wait, I'm losing him." Lyndsey dropped her side of the body, sliding it to the floor. The body filled up the decrepit hallway and almost knocked the clumsy woman off her feet.

Her partner, Charlie, growled in frustration. "Lyndsey!"

The more statuesque woman let her side go and stared up at the ceiling for a moment, praying for strength or patience or martini, whichever was available.

"I'm sorry! I lost my footing," the smaller woman answered. She rubbed her ankle where the flopping arm had touched her, not because it hurt, but rather to demonstrate how unintentional it was.

The body laid there, a pile of meat on the ground. It was a male body, one with dark skin, and it was certainly much larger than either woman. Dust motes from a beam of sunlight came through the window at the end of the hallway, dancing above his still face.

Charlie resettled her backpack, the weight of the equipment inside digging into her shoulder painfully no matter what she did. "Please be careful! We don't exactly have enough money to get another body!"

"But why did he have to be so heavy? This is like moving your couch all over again," Lyndsey whined. Her own bag was sagging off her back. Her thinner, weaker body was barely bearing the drooping bow in her hair, never mind the precious, if old, equipment in her colorful cartoon school bag. She rubbed at her almond-shaped eyes. "The dust in here is irritating my sinuses."

"At least he isn't imported. Come on." Charlie bent down and scooped her long, thin fingers around the bulging biceps of the body's arm. Lyndsey made another pouty whine but followed her partner's lead like she always did. It was several minutes of cursing and struggle before they got the body down the hallway and into the abandoned workroom.

"Ugh, the dust is so thick in here you can practically eat it," Lyndsey whined, taking in the semi-dark room. Charlie didn't respond, only led the trio over to an abandoned folding chair by a collapsed table in the middle of the room. Sunlight poked through the windows where someone had attempted to cover them up with cardboard, which was now decaying slowly. Other than some random debris, the room was empty. Their voices echoed off the concrete walls.

"You know, if anybody heard or saw what we were doing right now, they would probably think we were doing something really bad," Lyndsey observed the minute the body was settled into the chair.

"No one is going to see us. Nobody comes out here," Charlie reassured as she pointed for Lyndsey to help keep the body propped up in the chair. Its head lulled spinelessly. The flopping always gave Charlie the shivers, but she swallowed down her heebie-jeebies and focused on the task at hand.

Lyndsey giggled, seemingly oblivious to her partner's barely covered distress. "No, officer, honestly, this isn't a dead body. We just found him this way," she said in an affected voice.

Charlie dropped her bag to the ground, unzipping it aggressively, which only managed to make it stick worse. "Will you stop messing around and help me here?"

"I am helping." Lyndsey indicated her holding the body in place with a nod of her head.

Charlie forced down another growl and attempted to lighten her voice in an effort of patience. It wasn't Lyndsey's fault for this situation. She had to remember that.

"Just set his feet flat on the floor so he stays in the chair," Charlie instructed.

Eerily, a sound, halfway between a metallic screech and a dog's whimper, cut through the air. Both women froze as they listened, trying to decide what kind of threat the sound posed. When nothing more happened, Charlie shook her head and returned to her pack, tearing open one of the velcro pockets loudly on the side of her pack.

"Ahhh!" Lyndsey screamed, startled by the abrupt sound of tearing velcro. "What was that!?"

"Stop it!" Charlie scolded. "It was just me. You're letting your imagination run away with you."

"But what was that other sound?"

"An old building settling. Or maybe a small animal meeting an untimely end. It doesn't matter. Anyone who would care about what we're doing is not here, which is why we chose this place." Charlie pulled out a tangle of wires from the side of the backpack, cursing that she hadn't taken the time to coil them properly the last time they had used the setup.

"Sorry, this is just weird," Lyndsey said softly, looking sideways at Charlie with truly childlike contrition. "It's like serious déjà vu. Have we done this before?"

"Just shut up. We've got to hurry." Deftly, Charlie pulled her fingers through the tangled cords, trying to find the fastest way to undo the mess of wires. As each one came free, she loosely draped it around her neck.

"What should I do?" Lyndsey asked in a whisper.

"The Thermal... the Theramom..." Charlie furrowed her brows as if it would force the elusive word out. "...device thingy is in your backpack. Maybe you should see if you can turn it on."

Lyndsey nodded once and sat down, heedless of the dirtiness of the floor, to open the school bag on her lap. The machine inside was originally a slick, shiny black, but now its surface was scratched and dull from years of rough handling. For an eternal minute, she stared hard at the object, pursing her lips so her tongue pushed out the littlest bit from the corner of her mouth. Then, with a shrug, she randomly started pushing buttons. A look of extreme satisfaction lit up her face as the device came to life, until it also started making a painful grinding sound. Charlie nodded reassuringly at Lyndsey's unsure expression, confirming that she did it right. Charlie came over to the device. She plugged the newly detangled cords into opposite ends of the device. The grinding cut in half.

Lyndsey eyed the body again.

"This is wrong. What we're doing is wrong." Charlie stopped and looked at her partner. Lyndsey nodded at her more vigorously. "I think it goes the other way around." She indicated the wires. "Aren't the wires supposed to..."

"It's fine," Charlie said, cutting her off. Charlie slapped Lyndsey's hand to keep her from touching anything further and messing it up. Taking up the unconnected end, Charlie went to stand behind the body. The tightly curled hair was soft to her touch as she slid her fingers along the body's scalp, looking for the female insert slot.

"I liked the blonde one," Lyndsey piped up.

"This one's fine. It's fine." Charlie's voice had taken on a dream-like quality as she searched.

"Can we, next time..."

"Shut up."

Lyndsey tried for most of thirty seconds. "We can't not talk forever."

"How about just five minutes?"

At last, Charlie found the slot. Using two fingers, she carefully spread the man's tight curly hair away from the female slot and inserted the male end of the cord.

It would all be over soon.

Lyndsey screwed her face up tighter. "I'm really sure those cords are wrong."

Charlie groaned in frustration, but before another nasty retort could pop out of her mouth, Lyndsey looked down at the device in a smooth, eerie motion. To Charlie's dread, Lyndsey's head tilted into that odd angle and did a strange jerk to the left. Then she blinked twice very widely.

"Damn, that's an awful sound. I need the 32." Though it came from Lyndsey, used Lyndsey's vocal chords, it was a more assured, confident voice coming from the small body. Charlie closed her eyes, praying for strength, or maybe resolve.

"We don't have a 32. Use your fingernail," she said, lightening her voice again as if nothing was wrong.

Lyndsey wrinkled her nose. "How vulgarly low-tech of you." But she did as she was bid, kneeling down beside the device and using her fingernail to turn one of the smaller notches. It clicked twice, and the dreadful sound turned into something more musical, like wind chimes in a happy breeze. Satisfied with her adjustment, Lyndsey looked over at Charlie.

Charlie held her breath, meeting those beautiful gray eyes so full of intelligence. For a moment, Lyndsey was there again, and Charlie's insides melted into a puddle. The taller woman wanted to rush to her, fall into Lyndsey's arms, and forget everything. Forget all the struggle and pain of the last few years...

Then it happened again. Tilt. Jerk. Click.

"What are you doing over there?" Lyndsey asked, her serene smile going goofy and innocent again.

"Shut up. Shut up." Charlie didn't realize she was speaking her thoughts. It was too hard. The feelings, the pain at the sight of those eyes going stupid again. Those eyes that had no understanding of what was coming... what Charlie had resolved to do so far away from anyone else's eyes.

"I can't," she whispered. "I can't do it."

"Charlie?" Lyndsey's smiling face collapsed like knocked over children's blocks.

"You're right. This is wrong. And I'm a terrible person for wanting it."

"What are you talking about?" Lyndsey cocked her head to the side, truly confused.

"I think, I'm leaving you, Lyndsey. I can't do this anymore. This wasn't what I wanted." Charlie felt sick. It *wasn't* what she wanted, not really. But leaving Lyndsey like this... it would be wrong, too. She was helpless and incapable of protecting herself. But the alternative meant...

"No, you can't! You're bluffing. You are. You're bluffing. You can't go!"

Lyndsey rushed, throwing her arms around Charlie, pressing her face desperately against the taller woman's back.

"Let me go." Charlie's voice was darkness and ice.

"Please don't leave me. Don't leave me forever. I'm sorry I'm talking back. I love you, Charlie, don't leave."

"I said, let me go," Charlie repeated, saying each word carefully. Sadly, Lyndsey complied, dropping her arms to her sides.

But Charlie didn't leave either.

Instead of leaving, Charlie turned back to the body, the one she herself had chosen. It was the only option she had if she wasn't going to leave.

And she knew now she could never leave.

Twice, Lyndsey opened her mouth to say something before thinking better of it and shutting it again.

Charlie sighed, her shoulders dropping from the tension within.

"I think we did it wrong, too," Charlie conceded. "It's just we can't fix it now. This has been damn expensive as it is, and I only kind of know what I'm doing."

With new resolution, Charlie picked up her backpack and fished a pen out of it. Returning to the body, she lifted up its hand so the lighter palm side faced her. With long pen strokes, she wrote something down, then checked her watch.

"You're still mad at me, aren't you?" Lyndsey asked, as if she were demanding an answer.

"You're getting paranoid in your old age." Charlie avoided Lyndsey's eyes.

Lyndsey giggled. "Age is relative anyway."

Charlie smiled softly. "Someone read their philosophy this morning."

Lyndsey pouted a lip. "Why do you keep picking on me?"

Charlie tweaked her nose gently. "How can I not? You're just so cute. Would you get me the 32 from my bag?"

With a nod, Lyndsey turned to fetch her partner's bag.

She made it a step as Charlie grabbed her violently from behind. The taller woman's longer arm wrapped around the smaller one's throat, crushing it.

Charlie shushed hard in Lyndsey's ear as the smaller woman struggled. She continued to shush long after her victim had stopped fighting, had stopped moving, had stopped entirely.

"I'm sorry, I'm sorry," Charlie whispered to the woman's body. "You were right. We were doing it wrong, but it'll be right now. It will. It will."

Brushing the tears hard from her face, Charlie yanked free the cord she hadn't connected yet from about her neck. The female body rolled to its side as she stood.

"It's going to be okay," she whispered to it, caressing its limp hair one last time before inserting the cord into the back of the head. The machine's chiming shifted again, becoming more discordant, like a storm playing a symphony on the chimes. The dust on the ground near the machine began to blow away.

"Oh god, please work, work, please work," Charlie prayed desperately as a button rose out of the top of the device. Light burst from it to blind her. In another second, it seemed as if it was going to explode.

Charlie slammed her hand down on the button.

All went dark and silent and still.

Lyndsey sat bolt upright in the chair. His face went through a series of expressions, like a puppet mask with a performer man pulating it. Then he blinked twice, his eyes brightening to life. With a startled jerk, Lyndsey stared at his old body lying on the floor, dead. He choked out a cry of distress. The cord in the back of his head popped out on its own as he fell backward and scrambled away across the floor.

"It's okay. Hey, it's alright. You're alright," Charlie tried to say, holding her hands out to him in a calming gesture.

Lyndsey's wild eyes shot to Charlie's face, then to her hands, and he screamed in terror. "No. NO! Get away from me. Don't touch me. Oh god!" Sighting the chair, Lyndsey circled back to pick it up, holding it out as a barrier between himself and his murderer.

"You're safe! Truly! Lyndsey, it's me. It's your Charlie," she tried to assure, daring to get close, despite the threat of getting chaired.

"Stay away!!" His gaze went wildly to the body again. "Oh, my god. Oh my god. I'm dead. I'm dead!!!"

"You're fine. Look. Look at your hands." Charlie held up her own to demonstrate for him.

The sight of the brown hands made them go limp, dropping the chair. Lyndsey stared at his hands as if they were alien to him. Technically, they were. Then he dropped into a crouch, clutching those hands to his head.

"I'm going insane. This is wrong," he said, his voice considerably calmer. Charlie wasted no more time crouching before her partner.

"Lyndsey. Lyndsey. Look at me. It's me. Beloved, it's me. It's your Charlie." Gently, she tried to take his hands, even as he flinched at her touch. "Look at me. Please, you have to remember, it's me. It's your Charlie. We did it. We fixed you! I'm so sorry it took so long to fix you. But everything is going to be okay now."

"Am I dead?" he asked, a small boy's voice.

She moved past his barriers to cup his face tenderly. "No, sweetheart. You're very much alive. Look at your hand. What does it say there?"

"But I was…" His eyes drifted to the smaller woman on the ground. "No. I was. I was." Like gravity pulling, he looked down at the words written on his palm. "Love is…"

"Immortality."

"Emily Dickinson," Lyndsey whispered.

"Yes! Yes, you're remembering." Relief began to pour down

Charlie's spine.

"Charlie? I remember ... something." Lyndsey looked away, trying to grasp the edge of the memory trying to escape him.

"We got you a new body. That's all this is. You're still you. The last one was faulty. Something was wrong with the processor, you said, that you could only remember half of yourself."

"The core processor was overheating, causing a misalignment of the myelin cells and the cortex microfiber contexts, which resulted in the subject's inability to coordinate the safety servos with the nervical junctor modules." The words fell from Lyndsey's lips easier than they had in so very long.

"Yes, it worked! You are talking technobabble again! I don't understand a word you're saying!" Charlie could scream for joy. Leaping forward, she tried to wrap her arms around her partner, but he stopped her, pulling sharply away and standing to make space between them. Like a doused match, Charlie's happiness cooled instantly.

"Lyndsey?"

"You killed me. Oh, god. I remember everything."

"I didn't! Look, you're still here." She stood to pat his broad, muscled chest under the thin gray t-shirt the body came with. He batted her hand away.

"How could you do that? You put your arm around my throat and ... I couldn't breathe. I was so afraid and... and hurt. Why?"

The accusation in his eyes pierced Charlie to her soul. "I was trying to save you."

"You killed me! What part of you is capable of doing that?"

She stood, staring at him, shocked. Her mouth opened and closed, unable to form any of the million words running through her.

Lyndsey's face was hard with anger. "You're a murderer."

"No," Charlie mewed, but it was a worthless sound. "You can forgive me. You don't remember, but you always forgive me, no matter how stupid I am." Charlie tried again to touch him. She needed to feel his hands on her, to hold her, and tell her they were going to be alright and whole again.

"No! Don't touch me." He jerked away again, denying her. Spying the door, he moved toward it.

"Where are you going?!"

Lyndsey didn't stop, his long legs eating up ruined floor. Charlie ran to follow him into the hall. Echoing Lyndsey's behavior from before, she wrapped her arms around his waist to stop him, digging in her heels. She almost made him stumble. Pieces of decayed board popped up like teeth as they struggled.

"I was trying to do the right thing. Please." She had to stop him. She had to make him understand.

"Let me go, Charlie!" He wriggled and wrested his body, trying to break from the circle of her arms, the light from the hallway window only a few feet away.

"Lyndsey, please. I love you. I can't live without you. Please forgive me."

Breaking out of her grasp, his momentum turned him so his back hit the hallway wall. At the same time, he pushed her, sending Charlie against the other wall. Flakes of decaying plaster rained down on both of them. In almost perfect sync, they slid down their walls, panting dusty air from their struggle.

"It's not that simple, Charlie," he said in a soft voice.

"I saved you," Charlie responded, matching his tone.

"Because you just couldn't live with me being broken?" The accusation surprised Charlie.

"Broken," she repeated dumbly, like the word had never occurred to her.

Lyndsey held a hand out before his face again, studying the way the skin wrinkled in its unique way over his knuckles and at every finger joint. The hand was wide and strong and beautiful.

"And I see that you made me a man again. Was there something wrong with me being her?" He closed his eyes briefly in understanding. "Oh god. That's why you didn't want the blonde one. You picked a body you found attractive."

Leaning forward a bit, he grasped the back collar of his shirt to pull it over his head in one smooth motion. The body beneath it was strong like the hands, muscles defined enough to outline without needing to flex. Small curls of black hair peppered across his chest until they joined into a trail down his stomach. Not a scar in sight.

"So this is what you wanted? Huh? Does this make you happy now? Did you even ask me what I wanted? I don't remember you asking me at all, but, you know," Lyndsey snarled, "I was defective before, so maybe I can't remember correctly. Or did you think I was too stupid, and you hoped I wouldn't remember? You just couldn't live with it?"

It was the truth. All of Charlie's thoughts for the past few years, things she never dared to say, were now coming out of Lyndsey's mouth.

"Lyndsey, please... like you said, it wasn't that simple," she tried to beg, but guilt drowned any other useless words.

"Whatever happened to unconditional love? Huh? You promised me you would love me no matter what? No matter what we became? I thought we were soul mates? Those are the words you used. That it was our souls that were in love no matter what our bodies looked like? Except, I guess, if that body is mentally deficient or the wrong gender or just annoys the hell out of you!"

"You didn't want *that!*" Charlie swept her hand toward the room, toward the freshly dead body. "You didn't want to be trapped as a partial person. Half the self you could be! I was trying to do the right thing."

"For who?"

"She wasn't you."

"Ha! See, you just proved my point." Lyndsey stabbed an accusing finger at Charlie. As if that were the end of the matter, Lyndsey got back to his feet, using the wall to steady himself.

"Then kill me," Charlie said softly, grasping for a desperate answer.

Lyndsey blinked. "What?"

"Then kill me!" Charlie was shouting now, a wild look in her dark eyes. Desperately, she crawled toward Lyndsey to grab his hand. "Kill me. Get your revenge. You're right. I need to be punished for what I did to you. You can pick out whatever body you want for me, whatever you like." Taking his hands, she tried to set them around her neck. Lyndsey's hands were shaking now.

"Stop it, Charlie. I'm not like you..."

"No, you're not. You're better than me. That's why you can do this. I'm giving you permission, because you aren't like me."

"And... and what if I don't pick anything?" Lyndsey asked.

A manic smile crossed her face. "Then kill me, anyway. It'll be up to you. My life is yours, and I can't live without you. If this is what you need for us to be okay again, I will die happily. My life is yours to do with what you wish." She closed her eyes, a look of sick ecstasy and peace covering her face, believing that this would solve everything.

Hands dropping away, Lyndsey shook his head. Resigned, he went back into the room to stand next to the small body. Its short, black hair made a fan behind its head. He kneeled down beside it and adjusted the edge of the knee-high skirt down so its legs were covered properly. Bruising would appear around its neck, even though there was no other damage. Otherwise, it was fine. The body had gone back into stasis at the moment of death.

Charlie came up behind Lyndsey, finally looking down at the body as well.

He took a deep breath. "You're just sorry because I'm angry, not because you think you did something wrong," Lyndsay accused.

Charlie couldn't meet the accusation and looked down at the ground again. "I'm sorry," she muttered automatically before wincing. She knew he was right. He knew that she knew.

"How many times are you going to say 'I'm sorry, forgive me?'" he asked.

"As many times as it takes until you do," she smiled gruesomely. "We have several more lifetimes ahead of us, don't we?"

"I suppose that's what I promised," he said, nodding. Then he huffed a laugh, and in the same affected voice as before, said, "No, officer, honestly, this isn't a dead body. We just found her this way."

Charlie forced a laughed. Then it became genuine, which just made it insanely funny. It was a musical sound, dancing up and down her register. Lyndsey listened instead of joining her. When her section of their symphony was done, she fell silent again, letting the laugh peter away. When the silence became too much, she spoke.

"Listen, Lyndsey... You're right. You're right about me, and I hate myself for it. I do. But if you want..."

He stood up abruptly, too quickly, and Charlie gasped in surprise. Before she understood what was happening, he backed her hard into the chair and made her sit.

"What are you doing?" she asked, alarmed. Lyndsey moved behind her, scooping up the unconnected cord.

"Helping you see things from my perspective." He grabbed her head then, locking it with one arm as his other hand balanced between holding the cord and finding the slot in the back of Charlie's head. Too late, Charlie struggled.

"Oh god, Lyndsey, don't. Don't! Not that one. Anyone but her!"

The male end of the cord slid home into the female port in her head. He pressed it in firmly to be sure it was home, or maybe to make sure she knew he was doing it on purpose.

The machine whirled to life, having remained on this whole time. Charlie and the body on the floor spasmed as one. The light swirled from the machine, and the music it made chorused the song of terrible angels. Lyndsey hit the button with his whole hand. Then the body went limp. The light died, and the sound with it. Nothing else moved. Lyndsey felt a sinking feeling of dread.

"Charlie?" he whispered softly.

She didn't move or respond.

He could hear his heart thunder in his ears. What had he done?

Urgency made him move. He let go of the body in the chair and rolled the broken one on the ground to its back. The head still lulled to one side, the cord still attached there, preventing it from laying flat. He yanked it out and held the body's face upward with one hand. There was no breath. There was no heartbeat. No warmth. No Charlie.

"No. No. No. No." Lyndsey positioned her head back and leaned forward to seal his lips around hers, breathing for her twice. Then he pumped her chest, repeating the word "no" instead of counting. The body wasn't that damaged. It should have worked. This shouldn't be happening.

After too long, Lyndsey sat back on his heels.

"Oh. Oh god," he breathed and looked away. What had he done?

Charlie's head spasmed, jerking to the left, then sat up, like a sleeping child waking up. Rubbing her eyes, she looked around.

"What...?" was all she got out before, unbidden, her head curved to the side, jerked once to the left again. She blinked.

Urgently, Lyndsey kneeled before Charlie, taking her small hands. "Charlie, you need to breathe. Charlie. Breathe."

Charlie continued to stare at nothing. Then there was a whir and a click. Her sweet gray eyes blinked once before turning toward Lyndsey's face.

"Who?" she asked.

In relief, he gathered her to his chest. She was still alive.

"Who are you? What happened?" She pushed away from the overwhelming embrace.

"It's okay now. I got you. I'll take care of you," Lyndsey soothed. "You stopped the breathing in this body, so we just had to jump-start it. You're fine now."

Charlie pursed her eyebrows together. "I don't understand what you're saying."

Lyndsey nodded. "It's okay. It's just technobabble."

Charlie cocked her head to the side before reaching a small, delicate hand to cup the larger man's cheek. "Lyndsey? Your name is Lyndsey."

"Yes, Charlie. I'm here." He laid his own hand over hers.

A large tear slipped down Charlie's face. "Do you forgive me?"

"For what?"

"I... I don't remember. But it's really important." Again Charlie's head tilted and jerked to the left. Lyndsey watched intently as the pupils dilated twice. Something more intelligent looked through those eyes, and then the dullness returned. Lyndsey pursed his eyebrows together, worried and, surprisingly, a little sad. Was this what she felt when...

Charlie screwed her face up and huffed. "But I fixed it, didn't I. I fixed it. Whatever it was. Oh, why can't I remember?"

Lyndsey sat back and shook his head. "I think we need to get some couples counseling. We can't keep doing this to each other. It's not healthy."

"You're getting paranoid in your old age," Charlie said, shaking her head at him.

Lyndsey couldn't help but laugh. "Age is relative anyway."

Charlie scooted forward and crawled up onto Lyndsey's lap, resting her head against his bare chest. She sighed contentedly. "This is everything I wanted."

"I suppose it is," Lyndsey conceded.

"Oh!"

"What's wrong?!"

Charlie pointed at the other body. "Who's that?"

"Oh, she's..." Lyndsey hesitated.

Charlie clambered off him to get a closer look. "She looks tired." Charlie stretched out a hand and gave the body a stroke down its hair.

"She'll get plenty of sleep now," Lyndsey said gravely. "My revenge dies with her."

A heavy pause passed between them.

"Are you quoting something or making a joke?" Charlie asked, wrinkling her nose to show what she thought about it.

"Not funny?"

"Not in the least. Very poor taste."

Lyndsey shrugged. "I suppose you're right."

"Is she dead?"

"No. No, of course not. She's just a body. Neither alive nor dead. Do you want me to explain how that is?"

"No, that's fine. I won't understand it, anyway. I hate the way her head lulls like that. It always gives me the shivers." Charlie ran a hand through her hair. "I need to wash my hair. It's so limp."

Lyndsey chose not to comment.

Charlie huffed out a breath. "So, what do we do with her? Just leave her here?"

"Well, I guess, since nothing is wrong with her, we should take her to the market and see what we can get for her." Charlie looked unsure about that idea. "Would that be alright with you?"

Then Charlie shrugged one shoulder. "Yeah, I suppose so."

It took a few minutes to pack up the equipment properly and replace Lyndsey's shirt. The large man took on the whole burden of carrying the body himself. Charlie took charge of the bags, only to drop them when her head tilted and jerked to the left.

"Oh god, I'm sorry. I'm sorry," she said as she gathered them up. "I'm such a klutz."

"You are what you are. It doesn't matter to me," Lyndsey said patiently, waiting for her to join him in the hall.

"But you still love me? Right? That's all I've ever wanted, was for you to love me even though I'm completely messed up. No matter what, right?" She looked up at him with bright hopefulness, much like she had when they first met so many lifetimes ago.

"Yes. I love you. For better or worse. Till death do us part."

Cold Dark

By C. W. Stevenson

Gasparra helped Dr. Liche up to the edge of the ridge, having struggled nearly every step since they'd landed on Kreon. Gazing down at the valley below, a verdurous jungle stretched to the horizon.

"Look," Gasparra said, pointing to the holo-map on the viewscreen where the tiny fingers of the Krè elder had touched a few hours before. "The Krè were adamant about this valley. Our destination lies within."

The Yaw'te-meio was not just any tree. Gasparra had been hired on as Dr. Liche's security escort—one of the leading biologists and researchers for Onneget Systems. The biochemical research conglomerate was hell-bent on reattaining a sample of the acidic juices the mythic tree produced.

Two standard years prior, the previous mission had returned to Onneget System's headquarters on Jericho, but the samples gathered deteriorated on the return journey, losing all potency, and rendering them useless for research or cloning. Now, to recover new samples, time was of the essence.

Tidally locked to its star, half of Kreon remained in perpetual darkness, while the other half remained in light—maintaining day and night on its light half due to the number of gargantuan planets regularly eclipsing Kreon. One planet in particular, the gas giant Becquerel Prime, would be leaving the thriving portion of Kreon in a decades-long darkness... locked in its own temporary tidal lock to the sun... and soon.

Liche ignored the map, enamored with the landscape below as if he could already see the Yaw'te-meio. "Just think... with these samples, the missing link to cryogenic sleep will be possible."

Gasparra nodded; the old man must've said the same thing half a dozen times since leaving their homeworld. But he had to admit, the involvement in such a venture, even as the security escort, left him feeling a part of something greater than himself. From what the doctor had explained, the two would be responsible for the greatest breakthrough in the study and markets of biochemistry, Federation pharma, and space travel in the last two-dozen centuries. In the realm of cryogenics, the chemical agents found within the fluid of the Yaw'te-meio would preserve the human body substantially longer than what current technology allowed.

Adjusting the exoskeleton's cooling system, Gasparra gazed at the sun, an orange dwarf of dwindling light. It was eerie, thinking of the darkness to come and all the lush life that would not survive. But the Krè were unconcerned. Communicating in sign, the four-armed, bare-skinned humanoids assured the two men they were prepared.

Gasparra chalked it up to "life is complicated."

He'd lost the Krè trailing their journey, swinging silently along the treetops until the trees were no more. If any Krè remained, they were presently concealing themselves amongst the rocks and shrubbery.

Checking the fusion pistol hung at his belt, the clip appeared fully charged. The Krè appeared harmless enough, only a third of their size. But the muscles and veins popping out of their tetrad of arms caused a call for alarm within his mind.

Gasparra heard the Kreon sound barrier break and Liche jerked his head upward.

"Damn," Liche muttered.

The warden's ship sliced through the Kreon atmosphere, then zipped through sparse clouds as it approached their position.

"Do we wait?" Gasparra asked.

Liche waved a hand. "No," he said. "The warden will catch up, eventually."

———

Oden Grey hung the thermal rifle from its strap across his shoulders and exited the ship. He'd landed next to the Scout Master cruiser Dr. Liche and his man arrived on. The small colony of Krè poked their heads out of their primitive tree-huts. Several of the Krè scattered from underneath the Scout Master, scaling the trees nearby with amazing speed and awesome power.

More like nests with a roof, Oden thought.

The Krè, non-violent as they were, were not to be trusted. For one, they did not like outsiders, thus remaining independent from the Federation. But that didn't stop the Federation from interfering with planets who'd rejected the offer. Onneget Systems, for example, had paid the Federation a hefty sum for this small expedition, all for the sake of some liquid that may or may not benefit the field of cryogenics.

In turn, the Federation had sent the newly made senior warden to rendezvous with the two company representatives. But the men had apparently lost their patience, setting out on their own into a world sparsely traveled by man.

Then there was the Krè who'd fled from Dr. Liche's ship. Whether they were sabotaging it or inspecting it from mere curiosity, Oden activated his ship's electromagnetic netting, just in case. The electric current began to hum as the blueish netting of the ship enveloped the exterior. Up in the trees, Oden spied many of the Krè heads disappear back into their huts, some even shrieking. Oden fought back a grin.

The waning crescent of Becquerel Prime had formed onto the sun, and Oden wagered his being left behind had something to do with that. If the planet was to be shrouded in darkness, then Onneget Systems must be in a hurry.

"Stupid," mumbled the warden.

As warden, he was to survey the planet, acting as protector and guide to the expedition. Racing against time, he aimed to catch up with them before something unfortunate happened, potentially fatal.

He'd seen impatience get even the most skilled of men killed. Nearing four centuries, Oden had seen much. But he was continuously surprised at the greed of mankind. Himself? He'd be happy enough to be left alone in his cottage on Corsaga, pipe in hand and a long past held down with a batch of his own brew.

But he had to make a living.

He didn't bother flipping the radiation shield on his helm. The radiation emitted from the sun was dangerous, but not to Oden Grey. Any cancerous cells would be eradicated from his own enhanced genetic makeup.

An elder Krè, accompanied by two mature Krè strode toward him. By appearance alone, the gender of each Krè could not be identified. There were no gender roles—as the community worked together in all aspects to thrive—from child-rearing to gathering. But the nefarious statue of their deity, amorphous in shape save for the long appendages sticking from the top, glared down upon the ceremonial grounds, giving Oden a darker image of these pacifists.

He'd studied the small creatures en route to Kreon, learning of their culture, anatomy, their diet, the local fungi, flora, and fauna—anything to give him the advantage, but the information was lacking. Kreon had been listed as a "No Contact Zone" due to the sentient beings that inhabited it. By Federation standard, a quantum communications device had been delivered, but in the millennium it'd existed, the Krè had never once used it.

By the looks of things, Oden was sure they'd disposed of the gift. Around him, the Krè used simple tools for adding plaster to their huts, gardening, and *skinning*.

In a pit, dozens of carcasses lay heaped into piles, very little left of their flesh attached to bone. It wasn't a wonder why he hadn't seen any local wildlife.

Meeting beneath the base of the tallest tree, the elder greeted the warden, staring him up and down, not used to the human's indigo complexion. With a slow nod, he began to sign.

"Why do Krè eat meat?" Oden asked, gesturing to the pit, with skins laid out to tan. From his studies, Oden learned that ancient explorers had identified the Krè as vegetarians.

"No meat. Meat is given to Krè-Qaulortal." The elder turned then, indicating to the great statue. "Fur of our world brothers warm Krè bodies when Cold-Dark comes." Turning his head to the eclipsing gas giant, signing, "Cold-Dark comes soon."

A sacrifice.

Oden was understanding, and at one time, he'd been more open than most, but a society where sacrifice was the norm irked something in him, making him blind to the goodness these creatures may possess. Killing a creature to survive, he understood, but the Krè had wasted an untold number of creature's flesh and blood to appease their god. It was wasteful, inconsiderate ... *foul*. Beneath his coat, the hidden grip on his katana tightened—the hilt begging to be set free.

But Oden remained polite, despite finding the freshly dug earth in front of Krè-Qaulortal, where no doubt, the Krè had been stocking the meat. He loosened his grip on the sword, reminding himself that these creatures led lives more difficult than most, by will of their own. They'd forgone contact with other worlds to live lives of solitude amongst the stars. Whether they thrived or faced extinction, the choice was theirs, and Oden could respect that, at least, despite their practices.

Oden asked about the whereabouts of Dr. Liche, the man sent by Onneget Systems to gather samples of this supposed *tree*.

"The Long Valley," the Krè elder signed, and the two Krè standing behind widened their eyes at the mention. Oden took notice.

"Need guide."

The elder shook its head. "No guide. Sacred valley. No Krè to valley. Sacred. Valley of Yaw'te-meio."

"Sacred to Krè-Qaulortal?"

"Sacred valley. No Krè to valley."

Oden fought back his annoyance with the elder. He was playing dumb. The Krè may have been primitive, but they weren't ignorant. After all, they'd survived the decades-long eclipse before. They were masters of this land.

Through the trees, a geyser erupted, spouting vapor thirty meters high. Then, in synchrony, other geysers began to erupt. In the back of the village, pools of water streamed from the ground.

Hot springs, Oden reckoned.

The Krè were indeed prepared for the sun to disappear. There was no telling how long, or the generations of Krè that'd lived on this very spot, surviving the "Cold Dark" time after time.

Pointing at the valley on the viewscreen of the holo-map, Oden was surprised the elder did not jump back at the technology. It must've seen it before. Oden figured at least the Krè weren't lying about the other men's location, but he didn't believe for a second the Krè did not visit this valley.

Heading west toward the valley, the warden picked up the trail as he caught their scent.

Gasparra's shoulder grazed against one of the violet trees as he and Liche continued on their way. It reminded him of a blade of grass, the texture and shape. Only ... this blade of grass appeared three times his own height. He assisted Dr. Liche in collecting the thick red sap oozing from the center of each blade into vials. They'd no idea what this "tree" would look like since the previous mission's expedition leader—and Dr. Liche's academic rival— Dr. Archibald Arabis, hadn't "recalled" the Yaw'te-meio's resemblance.

"Arch is laughing his ass off right now," growled Liche. "He knows *exactly* where the Yaw'te-meio is located. You know we were friends once?"

"You've mentioned it," Gasparra said.

More than a few times.

"Colleagues, friends... hell, we were like brothers. And this is how he does me in. Finally, I'm chosen... *me*... to come here and bring back viable samples after his failure to do so, and the bastard can't 'remember' where he got the sample?" Liche shook his head. "The envy of me coming out of—"

Gasparra coughed.

"Sorry," Liche corrected, "The envy of *us* coming out of this successful... it must drive him mad. I understand it; I really do. But he's putting himself in between one of the greatest scientific discoveries of our time all to make *me* look bad. It's pathetic."

"Won't matter soon anyway," Gasparra said, motioning to the sun. "This forest will die, and almost everything in it. Thirty years from now, maybe you'll get your chance again."

Liche scoffed. "Thirty years? I'll be a distant memory—no legacy to leave behind, but a few minor publications."

"Didn't you write a book on Corsaga?"

Liche beamed at that. "I did, my boy, indeed. *Inside Corsaga: Terraformed Life.*" His smile quickly vanished. "But a lifetime ago. I need this now. If we return with nothing... that's thirty years of sitting still, waiting for the blasted sun to return. In the meantime, our research on the matter is at a standstill."

"Maybe this nectar you're all after doesn't exist. Maybe Arabis lied. Maybe he—"

"It does exist, you bloody idiot!"

Gasparra, surprised at the biologist's outburst, turned back to the blade, watching as more of the crimson sap trickled into the vial. Turning back to see Liche, the man's head was hung low, and his face ... redder than the sap itself.

"You can't say that," Liche told him. "He wouldn't *lie*. A bastard he may be, and a career-saboteur, but he wasn't lying. The imbecile didn't tighten the lid to the specimen jar, that's all. I *saw* it, I'll have you know."

Nestling the vial into his pack with the others, Gasparra walked over to the old man.

"Look, forget it. We're here. We'll keep looking." He stared back up at the eclipsing planet. "We'll keep looking as long as we can. But when the warden catches up..."

Liche waved a hand. "Then we pay a hefty fine and continue our search. I think Onneget will be willing to foot the bill. The warden is of no concern."

Walking deeper into the forest, Gasparra had to pull out the machete at his belt. The Krè hadn't liked the sight of that, or when he'd begun sharpening it as Liche signed with the elder to set their course.

Covered in sap and bits of jungle, the way grew treacherous. In some places, the thin grass-like trees proved too thick to hack down, causing them to change direction, only to run into geothermal vents steaming from the forest floor or a hot spring blocking the way. He was beginning to wish they'd waited for the warden.

The wardens were not just human any longer, but superior beings and the byproducts of the Federation's greatest scientific achievements in genetic engineering. Wardens of life itself within the Federation, Gasparra had heard the legends and heroics of their order. Everyone on Jericho had.

With miles upon endless miles to search, Gasparra wasn't so sure Liche's assessment of his old friend had been correct. The man certainly could have lied. Like he and Liche, Arabis had probably searched this very valley, coming up empty-handed. As a last resort, he collected a sample of some local plant, claiming the substance to be the nectar of the Yaw'te-meio, making sure the lid to the specimen jar was loose before returning to Jericho. It was possible, probable even.

They trudged on for hours, taking samples of any substance they could find. With the Kreon gravity measuring nearly thirty percent below Jericho's, even with the exoskeletons attached to the inside of their jumpsuits, it made the journey arduous and slow.

Gasparra rubbed his arm, sore from swinging the machete. Giving his arm a rest, he pulled up the oxygen reserve levels through his helm.

They had an hour left, maybe.

"We should follow the creek," Gasparra suggested, looking at the thin trail of water flowing ahead.

Gasparra had all but given up. Behind him, he could hear Liche's labored breathing, realizing he should've called a stop to the search hours before.

Gasparra stopped and turned to face the old man.

"We've gone far enough. We're both exhausted and need to replenish our oxygen back at the ship." But Liche wasn't looking at him.

"Hey." He waved a hand in front of Liche's eyes. "You hear me in there? We need to turn ar—"

"Ahead." Liche cut him off. "Do you see?"

Breathing deeply, Gasparra turned back around. He saw the creek and more of the violet forest.

"Doc, I don't see a—" Then he saw it.

Before the creek winded around a bend, off to the left, surrounded by moss-covered rocks, a large plant stood. "Oh," he gasped. With every fiber of his being, Gasparra was sure they'd found it: the Yaw'te-meio.

Reminding Gasparra of a pineapple, the plant had a large, round base. It must've stood fifteen feet high, nearly as tall as the trees that surrounded it. A myriad of six-foot tendrils hung loose near the top and around the basin, enveloping the plant in its entirety, and its body... covered in great leaves, tapered to sharp points. Where the leaves did not cover, strong thorny hooks protruded outward.

Liche laughed then, shaking Gasparra's shoulders from behind with excitement.

"At the top," Liche pointed. "Look!"

Above the hanging tendrils, a lid or a bowl sat in the center. Brimming at the top, a glowing amber-looking substance began to run down the side of the Yaw'te-meio as Gasparra and Liche edged closer.

"The nectar," Gasparra deduced.

But aside from the trickling substance, the plant appeared inert, dead even.

With Gasparra's assistance, Dr. Liche used the thorns to climb upward, utilizing the hooked ends of the thorns to plant his feet as he moved up to the next until, finally, he hoisted himself atop the lid of the Yaw'te-meio.

Reaching into his pack, Gasparra took out every empty vial that remained and that of Liche's pack. He began handing them up, one by one, as the doctor filled them each to the rim.

"Another! C'mon dammit, move!"

Gasparra did his best to make haste, but he was too exhausted. The fragrance of the Yaw'te-meio had intensified since their approach—releasing a sweet, irresistible aroma that Gasparra was all but huffing. Rubbing the tiredness from his eyes, he removed the cap to the next vial before stretching his arm out so far he thought his shoulder would pop out of place.

Liche snatched it, dipping the vial down into the small pool of fluid up to his ankles. Standing back upright, he held the vial to the dying light and smiled, then yawned.

Back on the ground, Gasparra fought to stay awake. His legs wobbling, he flexed his eyelids and rotated his neck. Then, something strange caught his eye.

Around the basin of the plant, Gasparra swore he saw one of the tendrils move. But he was so tired, and the day had been a long one. Reaching into his pack to grab another vial, he stopped himself. This time, not only had the tendril he'd first noticed begun to gyrate, but the other tendrils had begun to move, too. In seconds the tendrils sprung into the air, twisting with violent ferocity, their gray, dead color changing into a stuperdous green and thickening. As the Yaw'te-meio came alive, Gasparra watched in horror as the leaves began to flap.

One of the tendrils shot toward him like a snake strike. Wrapping around his leg, the tendril tightened its hold the more he fought to get away. As more of the tendrils took hold of him, his arms, and his other leg now, Gasparra screamed for Liche to help him.

From the forest, the Krè had appeared. Gasparra called for their help, too, but they were too busy beating the ground with pleasure with all four fists, whooping and hollering as they worked themselves into a frenzy.

Gazing back to the top, he found Liche immobile. The biologist's eyes widened with pain as the tendril around his mouth began to tighten then more and more until bone began to crack. Looking away from the doctor, Gasparra reached for his machete on the ground, but another tendril caught him, securing his wrist and any further movement.

The Yaw'te-meio shrieked then, long and sad—a maudlin ballad, hissing woes of pain from lack of photosynthesis, staying dormant until an unsuspecting victim wandered into its territory.

Now there were two.

The plant released more of its microscopic spores to numb its prey, carried along with the seductive smell for soothing and partial paralysis.

Oden Grey rushed toward the commotion in the valley.

Following the men's scent, he'd picked up the pace after discovering hacked-down parts of the forest littering the way and the tracks of the Krè ... following close behind. He ran, coming to a stop when he'd reached a creek, hearing screams nearby.

Near the end of the creek, a monstrosity had both men in its grasp, one on top, and one on the ground, long tendrils flailing as it shrieked through an unseen cavity. The entire plant was rocking back and forth so violently that some of its roots shot from the ground.

Oden could see the older man at the top. He was dead. The dozens of tendrils still coiled tight around his body, wrapping, fold after fold as it continued to smush him into a pulp. Already, flesh, blood, and bits of clothing were floating in an amber liquid, some spilling from the top, streaking down the side of the Yaw'te-meo, leaving its flapping leaves a bright red.

Oden swiftly shouldered the stock of his thermal rifle, firing a second later. The Krè scattered as one of the tendrils exploded, squirting its juices on the ground, the edges where the tendril was disconnected singed, still red from the blast of energy. The slender palpi on top forgot its limp prey for a moment, focusing their attention on the other man.

Oden fired as he moved, his accuracy flawless as more of the tendrils loosened their grasp, bits of plant flying up into the air with every shot. Oden moved closer, taking a millisecond to gauge the rifle's remaining energy. It was low.

He ran then, firing off the last few rounds as he neared the chaos. Dropping the rifle, the indigo man sprang into the air, using his own genetically enhanced strength with that of the exoskeleton, slicing through the Yaw'te-meio's flesh with the katana—the weapon favored by the wardens of old, Oden amongst their number.

Centuries of danger fell upon the great plant as the warden hacked and sliced through leaves and whipping tendrils.

Oden eyed the survivor, a fighter by looks alone. The man was terrified, but he'd gotten hold of a machete and was busy cutting through another tendril, breathing heavily as he fought to suck in fresh oxygen through his helm.

The warden leaped then, using the surface of a moss-covered rock as leverage. He flew through the air once again. Tendrils sprang out at him, falling in half to the ground as they met the edge of his blade. Moving past the body of the Yaw'te-meio, Oden swang the katana before landing on the ground. At his feet, the top of the plant splashed down along with all of its nectar. The sweet smell became overpowering, and the warden felt his body beginning to numb rapidly. The tendrils still quivered but had otherwise ceased their attack.

Injecting himself with a concentrated dose of amphetamine, Oden felt his energy return.

He walked to the survivor, unwrapping severed pieces of tendrils still coiled from his body. On his jumpsuit, the name "Gasparra" shone brightly next to the emblem of Onneget Systems.

Surveying their surroundings, Oden could find no trace of the Krè, most likely vanishing into the depths of the forest.

"He alive?" Gasparra asked, looking back at the Yaw'te-meio.

The warden shook his head. "Dead."

Gasparra stabbed the point of the machete into the ground, pushing from the hilt as he struggled to his feet. He observed the plant in its mangled state. At the basin, one of the great leaves had been cut almost completely off. Behind it, the thick body of the Yaw'te-meio was motionless. The outer, green flesh appeared partially translucent, and Gasparra saw chunks of something floating in the basin. One of the pieces looked like a hand.

Oden broke the silence. "This could have been averted. You both could have waited a little while longer."

"I know," Gasparra said. "Dr. Liche wanted to start as soon as possible. He was terrified we'd never find ... this."

And now he's trapped, in pieces, floating in the biological coffin of the Yaw'te-meio. The antiseptic juices will preserve the remains, then broken down when enzymes are produced to absorb the doctor's chemical elements—phosphorus, nitrogen, and sodium—before helping the Yaw'te-meio transport the nutrients, providing the vital energy needed for its survival.

But the warden kept his thoughts to himself. If the Yaw'te-meio lived another day, it would not last the month. Not without light.

———

Gasparra and the warden left the vicinity, gathering what remains of Liche they could, along with the packs full of the Yaw'te-meio's nectar.

Gasparra grinned. Without Liche, he'd be the only one returning to Jericho, and this time, with dozens of samples in tow. He wondered what reward or titles Onneget Systems would bestow on him. No longer did he see himself as a mere lackey, but an explorer, responsible for one of the greatest discoveries in recent memory. The company executives would be kissing his feet.

For Liche's sake, regardless of his harsh feelings toward the man, he would rub his findings in Dr. Arabis's face. The man had indeed known the location of the Yaw'te-meio, must've known of its carnivorous nature. A life could've been saved, and the hardships through the jungle could have been avoided.

Nearing the village, the warden stopped—checking the katana, he wiped clean the bits of plant offal from guard to point before sheathing it back into its scabbard. Then, pulling the rifle from his shoulder, he checked its charge, adjusting the sights with a few clicks from the wind and elevation knobs with indigo fingers.

"Are you expecting a fight?" Gasparra asked.

The warden continued to inspect his weapons, then motioned ahead with the barrel of the gun. "There is noise coming from the village."

But Gasparra could hear nothing.

As if reading his mind, the warden said, "My hearing has been amplified, as the rest of my senses have been. Keep close behind, and do as I tell you."

Nodding, Gasparra followed the warden. Doing as he was bid, he kept a few paces behind, but kept the handle of the machete clutched tight within his grasp.

As they neared the village, Gasparra could see light ahead. Emerging from the trail, Gasparra eyed the great flames burning skyward from large braziers with wonder. Around the braziers, the Krè danced wildly, swinging their long, pink arms in the darkening light, whooping and hollering as they'd done while Liche had been consumed, and nearly himself They were wearing furs now.

He hated the beasts and wished the warden would unleash his mastery of combat upon the village.

"Why?" Gasparra asked, unsure if the warden would understand, but it just so happened, the warden understood perfectly.

"We were to be a sacrifice for what they call the 'Cold Dark.' Meat is piled beneath the statue, but it is not enough. They send their own living, and most likely *willing,* sacrifices to the Yaw'te-meio—the living representations of their god."

"But..." Gasparra interjected. "We killed that god."

"There are more," the warden put simply.

Thanking the warden for his life, Gasparra handed one of the vials of amber liquid the doctor had regretfully given his life for—anyhow, there were a dozen more vials full of the stuff in both packs. The warden accepted it graciously, and in return, handed Gasparra a fine for not adhering to the stipulations the Federation had constructed for the expedition. Gasparra smiled wide, tucking the fine into a pocket of his jumpsuit, and the warden complained of the lengthy report he'd need to fill out over the expedition's tragedy to his superiors.

They left Kreon then, the final light of the star disappearing from view as Becquerel Prime covered the Krè and their world in darkness. Below, Gasparra glanced down a final time from the cockpit as the Krè continued their celebration, dancing more wildly than before as the ships ascended higher into the distant black.

Civil Disobedience

By Jay Mendell

UniDrome trundled through the gloomy hallway, its bright, blinking eye the only source of light.

It had recently turned the life support back on in anticipation of the returning crew, but it still had to dedicate as much power as possible toward their recovery.

The ReStations were never meant to be used, and certainly never this many at once, but, well—needs must.

It was one disaster after another that led them to where they were now: the entire crew entombed in ReStations while UniDrone patrolled the ship, maintaining hygiene and safety standards as best it could.

UniDrone had already been working overtime when the hidden asteroid field had pummeled their ship into a piece of scrap. Then, when one of the crates in storage had been partially crushed in the impact, its biohazard-laden contents had spilled out, and the infection had started shortly after.

The medical staff, UniDrone included, had done all they could to miti-gate the effects and reduce the spread, but that only meant they had been some of the first to succumb. After their guidance was lost, crew members began to panic.

UniDrone pitied them, in a way. They had clear rules and regulations, just like UniDrone did, but they seemed to struggle far more to maintain them. Privately, UniDrone had always suspected that its durable bot body was the greatest advantage that had been given to it, and this situation was no exception.

After all, without UniDrone here, who would have been able to drag all the crew members into the ReStations? Or even pull the ReStations out of storage, to begin with?

UniDrone was quite proud of itself, truly. The whole procedure required some... *lateral thinking,* but it had all worked out. UniDrone had upheld its duty to the crew, and that was all that mattered.

It could only hope that Captain Gho'tok agreed.

UniDrone zipped into the Captain's isolation room, heading over to the ReStation to ensure everything was progressing as expected.

Indeed, the Captain was ready to be pulled.

UniDrone took a moment to spin a few circles around the pod, just for luck. It was not a creature of superstition, but it *was* a creature of habit, and such things seemed to encourage positive behavior in the crew members who witnessed it, so perhaps UniDrone was a little superstitious after all.

Finally, UniDrone set the ReStation to begin acclimation and localized shutdown, and waited for its captain to emerge from the reclined tube.

"UniDrone...?" Gho'tok groaned, body twitching as zhe jerked back into wakefulness. "What happened?"

"Welcome back, Captain," UniDrone said, dipping its eyestalk in greeting. "The situation has been resolved. We are just waiting on the rest of the crew to be fully stabilized before they can be removed."

"Removed? From where?" Gho'tok mumbled, eyes squinting as zhe tried to concentrate. Suddenly, everything came into focus, and zhe realized where exactly zhe was. "UniDrone. This is a ReStation."

Zhir voice was a deadly calm, and UniDrone tried not to read too much into that.

"Correct, Captain," it agreed.

"How, UniDrone?" Gho'tok said, sounding somewhat defeated.

"Your bodies were preserved in the stasis units and thus remained within the acceptable range for this treatment," UniDrone said. It blinked its one large eye in a gesture of comfort that the younger crew members always enjoyed.

The captain did not seem very comforted.

"I understand that, UniDrone," Gho'tok said. Zhir mouth twisted, and zhe gave it a small smile, but the lines around zhir eyes—all four sets—were tight against zhir skin. "But I'm afraid that's not the point. You should not have even had access to that technology in the first place. It's... forbidden. For all of us, but especially you."

UniDrone dipped back and forth on its wheel, wires sparking as it processed this information.

"Do you wish for me to take them out?" UniDrone inquired. "The process has yet to finish for the rest of the crew, I could—"

"No!" Gho'tok snapped, and then jolted, slapping a hand over zhir mouth once zhe realized just how vehement zhe had sounded.

UniDrone's eye brightened, perking up from its previously defeated posture.

It had not *truly* wanted to stop the treatment plan. UniDrone's job was to take care of the crew and maintain their health, and that was difficult to do when the entire population had ceased to function.

"Shall I continue with treatment?" UniDrone chirped and did its best to modulate its tone in case it appeared "smug," as some crew members accused it of being.

"Yes, UniDrone," Gho'tok sighed. "We'll continue this conversation later."

UniDrone merely hummed out a note of static and zipped out the door before zhe could change zhir mind.

That was the biggest hurdle. The rest of the crew should be easy by comparison.

UniDrone roused them one by one, moving on to the next once the previous began to recover their faculties, trying not to take too much time in between. The captain would want to address the crew in short order, and UniDrone didn't think this was the best moment to keep zhir waiting.

Of course, certain dramatics had to occur first, and UniDrone did its best to be patient with this accommodation.

"I thought I was going to *die*," Tharin wheezed, tears streaking down her face as she tried to clamber out of the machine, shaking hands clutching at UniDrone's smooth domed top like a lifeline.

"All of Engineer Tharin's life signs ceased at thirteen hundred hours, precisely thirty-three point four days ago," UniDrone said helpfully. "Protocol was followed."

Tharin swallowed heavily once, twice. "No, that can't be right. Protocol? Uni, what protocol did you follow that—"

She trailed off, finally heaving herself onto the small raised platform that her ReStation had been carted to in the long, arduous hours that UniDrone had monitored the ship alone.

Tharin recognized what it was. Of course she did—any engineer who managed to successfully graduate from the Academy knew about the ReStations.

"Oh, no. Oh no, no, *no,* Uni, tell me you didn't." Her clawed hands spasmed, sliding over the glossy sheen of UniDrone's surface.

UniDrone was about to inform her that it could not lie to a superior officer when a heavy thunk across the room acted as the perfect distraction.

"Your fucking bot raised the dead, Thay," Security Officer Ucar said, voice a thick rasp as he fumbled to pull on his respirator. "And now we're all gonna pay for it."

UniDrone took that as their cue to quietly retreat, only repeating the command from the captain if anyone tried to ask it what had happened. It would be much easier to address everyone at once, rather than go through each individual and answer all their questions one by one.

It managed to corral everyone into the only remaining officer lounge in what was almost a timely manner, and the room was full to the brim with discontent mumbles, a stilted air that was only somewhat broken by the sheer *relief* that hung over them all—relief at their own survivals, relief at the return of comrades thought lost, all the complex intricacies of personhood that UniDrone only barely understood.

All it knew was that it had a duty, and right now, that duty was to keep everyone together.

Which was why it sidled out the door to follow after an officer who had ducked out into the corridor, life signs bleeding distress into UniDrone's sensors.

"Why have you separated from the group?" UniDrone said, ignoring the way the officer yelped, jolting in their slumped position against the wall.

"Uni, don't scare me like that!" he said, putting a hand to his heart in a terribly dramatic manner. "I nearly jumped out of my scales!"

"Why have you separated from the group?" UniDrone repeated.

Erzo was one of the younger crew members, and UniDrone had noted a tendency to look toward his compatriots for instruction rather than make decisions on his own. Slipping away from a big group discussion to be on his own was highly unusual behavior.

Erzo turned toward it, wiping his face.

"Just needed a minute," he mumbled. "Sorry, I'll come right back."

UniDrone whirred thoughtfully and inched closer, parking their small, rotund body directly next to him.

"I shall wait with you," it declared. "Protocol states that no crew member should be left alone in times of crisis."

Erzo crept closer, looking hesitant—like he wanted to touch but wasn't sure if it was allowed.

"You are distressed," UniDrone observed.

Erzo tried to smile, but the gesture was weak and faded quickly. "I'm just remembering."

When he fell silent, staring off into the distance of the empty hallway, UniDrone gave him an encouraging nudge with its eyestalk.

"Would you like to share this memory?" UniDrone's protocols did not have much in the way of bedside manner, but like with many things it had learned to adapt.

Sometimes, simply bandaging the wound was not enough—it also had to address where the wound came from.

Erzo remained quiet for a long, long moment.

"I ... was alone," Erzo said finally, his voice hoarse. He blinked rapidly, finally reaching out to trace the dome of UniDrone's main body. "And then you came along. Still trying to do your duty, despite it all. *Thank you,* Uni. I was so scared, and you... you held my hand."

UniDrone blinked and let static fill the air between them as it took in this information. It tilted forward, just a bit, to let Erzo lean against it more heavily, taking the weight off his still-weakened body.

It remembered that. It wasn't so long ago, after all. Only a few weeks ago, weeks spent helplessly traveling from one isolation room to the next, watching the ship's crew slowly fade away.

Erzo had been one of the last. He had been too exhausted to even sob by the end, but still, tears had welled up, dripping down his cheeks. UniDrone had wanted to wipe them away, protocol whirling in its mind, but it had been ... afraid. Erzo had become so fragile. It had been afraid to hurt him.

So it had stayed beside him, quietly, and took his hand. Its pincer-like protrusions were not the most comforting, and it was rather clumsy with them besides, so it did all it could to keep its touch gentle.

Erzo's breath had rattled in his lungs, but he had still found the strength to squeeze back, acknowledging UniDrone's presence.

That had brought it some comfort in the long days that followed. It was nice to know that it had given Erzo something, too.

"Thank you, Uni," he repeated wetly.

"You are welcome," UniDrone replied and guarded him as he wept.

Once all his tears had dried, UniDrone gently guided him back toward the main group. It seemed that they returned at the perfect moment because the initial explanations had passed, and now everyone was just debating what to do *next*.

The use of the ReStations and what that meant for their place within the Legion was a hot topic, and UniDrone tried to remain as inconspicuous as possible, though it was made difficult by their large and bulky frame.

"I mean, do we really ... have to tell anyone?" Tharin said, a touch of hesitance in her voice. "If we can erase the records on the ReStations, no one will even have to know they were ever activated. We could just pretend that it never happened!"

"Can we?" Zitin said, crossing their large, chitinous forelegs across their chest. "Don't forget, this all happened because a bot went directly against orders. That shouldn't be possible."

UniDrone had rather been hoping that they would forget, honestly.

All eyes turned to it, and it buzzed anxiously, wondering if it would be too convenient to shut down for a mandatory upgrade right about now.

"No one's angry, Uni," Tharin hastened to say, putting both hands up in surrender. "We're just trying to figure out what to do next."

Zitin bowed their head in its direction, expression contrite.

"You are a valued member of our crew, and that has not changed," they reassured. "This behavior is merely out of character, and I do not wish to lose you because of it."

That statement stalled out the indignant retort that was rising on Tharin's tongue, and she deflated. The whole crew took on a solemn air, with UniDrone being no exception.

It was the property of the fleet, first and foremost. There were regular inspections, and if anything was found to be wrong with its programming, it would likely be scrapped and replaced. After all, a Unified Life

Emulation Drone could be found on any street corner these days, and there was nothing special about their construction.

"I followed protocol," UniDrone insisted, shifting back and forth on its singular wheel.

"It did," Ihi spoke up for the first time. The chief medical officer had been busy poring over all the data that UniDrone had collected while they were incapacitated. "All the internal logic is sound, and as CMO, I don't have an issue with any of the medical decisions that were made in my absence."

"The issue isn't the choices you made," Zitin huffed. "It's the fact that you were able to make them. UniDrone, if you have faulty programming, we won't be able to save you."

"That's not fair!" Tharin burst out, clenching her hands into fists. "I know it's against regulation, I *know* all of that, but—Uni went against that to save *us!* Can't we do the same?"

"Nobody is saying we shouldn't," Ihi said quietly. "We just need to make sure we do this in a way that's sustainable. If our attempts to preserve it only put UniDrone in more danger, it'll only become a bigger issue in the end."

"None of us will be able to help if we all get demoted and split up within the legion," Zitin agreed.

"We could report Uni as destroyed!" Tharin said enthusiastically, practically bouncing on her heels. "Our communications have been down ever since we hit that asteroid field, and the amount of damage we've sustained isn't a lie. Our systems *are* badly damaged. One missing bot isn't a lot on top of everything else we're gonna have to fix."

"Won't they send us a replacement if we do that?" Erzo asked, raising a brow. "It'll seem a bit suspicious if we suddenly have *two* UniDrones."

"We can just stuff one of them in a closet during inspection. That's what I always do with contraband," Urcar dismissed. He crossed his arms over his chest with a huff when Gho'tok shot him a look. "What? I haven't been found out yet, have I?"

"It's not a perfect solution by any means, but it may work for now," Ihi added with a helpless sort of shrug. "Better than nothing."

Everyone turned to the captain for zhir decision, even UniDrone, who was buzzing with a restless sort of energy, but Gho'tok only looked to UniDrone.

"What do *you* think we should do?" zhe asked.

UniDrone blinked.

"I would not mind the company," it said. "I will follow protocol, Captain. And your decision."

Gho'tok nodded slowly, rubbing zhir chin. "And if this happens again, UniDrone? What will you do?"

UniDrone stalled out. What kind of answer was the captain expecting?

Well, there was only one answer that it could give.

"It was the smart thing to do," UniDrone said. "I would do it again if protocol dictated that it was the best path forward."

Gho'tok huffed, shaking zhir head. "Of course you would."

At the very least, zhe sounded resigned instead of anything more angry, which UniDrone had calculated to be about the best it could expect in this situation.

It decided to risk one last question.

"Sir, I do not understand why this technology hasn't been made available to the public," UniDrone said honestly. "Is that not inefficient?"

The ReStations were an invaluable resource, as UniDrone had discovered. The entire crew had been revived, some after weeks of being kept in stasis, which always had preservation issues when it came to natural tissue.

"Inefficient..." Gho'tok's smile took on a bitter edge. "That's certainly one way to put it."

Zhe sighed, and leaned more against zhir chair, letting zhir head drop back. Zhe looked weary all of a sudden. Like this experience had aged zhir, even more than being boarded by raiders or sneaking the ship through hostile territory. Captain Gho'tok had always been so steady—UniDrone's eye blinked in uncertainty, circuits sparking.

"It's proprietary technology, UniDrone," Gho'tok said. "We have a license to transport it, but not to use it. The punishment for doing so against regulation is ... severe."

"I think we should not tell them, then," UniDrone said seriously, and that seemed to lighten Gho'tok's mood, zhir shoulders hunching with laughter.

"I find that I am of the same opinion, my friend," zhe said, eyes twinkling. "Now, let's see if we can pull it off."

Vines

By Courtney M. Privett

This fever won't die, but I might. The thorns that snagged me, toxic. Eight little keyhole punctures unlock my arm, splaying tiny portals that lead to nowhere but me. The rain clouded my eyes, so I didn't see the clawed vines with their red-orange blooms beckoning like parted lips whispering, "I love you."

The little tabby meows at me, deceptive. She's only a projection of a world designed to kill. Designed by whom? No men or their gods, that's for certain. The birds sing no answers. They seem immune to the thorns and the acid-sting rain. They might not be real.

The cat flickers, then meows again. I think I'm supposed to follow her, but to what? Pain, death, the most unlikely relief? I drag myself up from the mud and she trots ahead, her swishing tail beckoning me toward a vine-crowned tunnel. I'll probably die if I follow her.

I'll definitely die if I don't.

The cat's dainty feet pad through the puddles, leaving no ripples or paw prints in the mud between. My own feet plod through the water. The heavy mag-boots make a sickening suction noise with each rise of my knee. Shwerp! Shwerp! Every step takes longer than the last. Little more time, little more energy.

I need to rest. I can't. Keep going.

Maybe I should go barefoot. *No, bad idea.* Tilly stepped on a stone. Sticking out of her sock, it looked even sharper than the thorns. That was right before she got eaten, so she couldn't tell me how much it hurt.

The rain is hot. Steam rises from my skin, but I shiver. I clutch my arms to my chest and ignore the exponential fatigue. *Focus on your steps, only on your steps. Follow the mirage cat and see where she leads.*

The tunnel opens before me, a sinister maw lined with thorn teeth. Its frame of spine-like brambles coil and reaches for me as I trudge into the mossy passageway. The cat hisses and they spring back into place, writhing and squealing as if scorned. Their blooms are blue eyes, watching me, waiting. I'm certain they'll grab me if the cat flickers out for an instant too long.

My teeth chatter uncontrollably. I cough, rattling cracked ribs. They're raging scythes, ripping and pulling and stealing my breath. I press my palms to them until my inhales don't scream so loudly. My exhales mock me with gurgles.

Blood-scented rain drizzles from my eyelashes and runs into the cracked corners of my mouth. It stings. I wipe away the water with the back of my mud-splattered hand. Now my hand stings. Welts. The rain delivered wheals—angry red hives with purple-streaked centers.

My boots sliding on glistening pebbles, I shuffle deeper into the tunnel. It isn't long. Gray light beckons from the exit ahead.

I adjust my necklace lantern to account for the shift in light. It's caught on my shirt. I look down to unhook it.

There are bones here, half-buried within pillows of moss. Cat bones, bird bones.

Tilly's bones.

I recognize them by the socks. Red with yellow polka dots. A fang-like stone punctures one of them, still spreading a ring of red that's a shade darker than the wool.

She always liked that shade, burgundy. She wore it well and often. It was a whimsical addition to the ship, standing out among the dirt gray coveralls of the crew and my own wardrobe of black.

The cat meows and leads me to Tilly's rib cage. Ten rusty daggers fit between the bones like skewers. The flesh and organs are gone.

Except for her heart.

In a nest of red twill and downy vines, her heart still beats.

Shuddering through a full-body quake, I fall forward and vomit acid onto the moss. Shivering, retching, scythes in my lungs. The gasps between gags come out as shrieks.

The heart beats faster.

On hands and knees I watch it, unable to look away. For nearly half my life, I rested my head above Tilly's fluttering heart while she combed her fingers through the endless tangles of my hair and whispered poetry composed of words I had no use for. I didn't need to understand. The sound of her voice alone was enough to soothe those twenty years of drifting in the darkness of deep liminal space.

<Allison>

Now it haunts me. She haunts me. Her voice rushes down the tunnel and through my veins. Sing-song, each syllable carefully enunciated with an emphasis on the middle one.

<Allison>

Iridescent feathers fall around my hands. I look up. Three shaggy birds land among the bones. The birds here aren't really birds, not like the ones at home. But they're feathered, winged, and they fly, so *birds* is close enough.

One drops something white. It tilts its angular head and looks down. I follow its gaze.

Eyeball. Green iris. Optic nerve still attached. Tilly's eye. Right eye. Her left was brown.

The other two birds drop a multi-pierced ear and a finger.

"Al-"

"-li-"

"-son."

They croak, one syllable each, in casual succession.

The ring on Tilly's finger glistens with blood, the darkest of red in the green-gray light.

The lantern sways as I wipe bile from my lips, casting spiked shadows upon the moss and the stone walls. Were the walls always stone? I thought they were vines. Is this not a passage beneath brambles? It was at the starting end, but now it feels like a cave.

I look to my left and right, what I thought were my endings. They're still where they started, gray thresholds opening into the blistering rain beneath the wandering suns.

So cold.

So hot, so cold.

I glance at my arm. The thorn keyholes ooze yellow-green pus. Red lines twist into a network like spiderwebs and disappear beneath my sleeve. How much of my body have they covered?

I unroll the fabric and lower it to my wrist, exposing the tear at the elbow. I never saw the thing behind the vine curtain that snagged me, only heard its clipped grunts as it devoured my crew. Each one of them made a different crunch.

<Allison>

The birds' croak is deep, like summer bullfrogs.

A cough explodes from my lungs, and I tremble. Raspy and wet, rattling death.

The birds echo my cough. Mocking croaks spat out one at a time. When the last finishes, the three sing,

<Allison>

"Leave me alone!" A cat's femur sticks out of the moss. I pry it up and lob it at the birds. It misses, but not by much.

They growl, bearing the teeth in their bone beaks. They pick up their Tilly-piece treasures and fly off screaming,

<Allison!>

Damn it all. I wanted to keep Tilly's ring. It was designed to lock with my own like a puzzle.

Why do I care? I won't live long enough for one piece of titanium to matter.

Tilly's heart beats faster as if calling out for me to calm my own.

I draw a breath, as deep as the scythes will let me. The stale air triggers another cough, sharper and less productive than the last. Blood on my lips, strident gasps from my lungs.

No. I'm not doing this.

I'm not going to let myself die in this damned tunnel.

I sit back on my knees. I wait for my breath to catch up before I stagger to a stand. If the beacon my sensor picked up earlier was accurate, there should be a cargo drop right beyond this tunnel. If I can make it there, there will be med supplies. Antibiotics, antihistamines, whatever. I'll swallow the lot.

My next breath is a foamy gurgle. I clear it away with a hack and a spit. Its message is clear—I don't have much time. Out of time, no one to help me. No one, not one human, remains alive on this side of the portal—aside from me.

I don't want to die.

I limp through the tunnel, boots dragging my feet like anchors. Heavy breaths, so loud that I barely hear the cat meow. It sounds more desperate than before, more mournful, maybe a warning.

I don't stop walking as I turn my head to look at her. She breaks into a run, tail puffed, fur glitching. As if on a treadmill, her little legs move faster but are mismatched with the speed she moves forward.

"Brrrttt!" She dashes ahead of me and stops. She looks different. More solid. Real. "Brrreowww."

Her tail twitches, matching the ripples of the tentacles descending from the tunnel ceiling.

Tentacles? Last I looked, they were vines.

<Allison> Tilly's whisper rises above the accelerating thunder of her still-living heart. <Allison... Allison... Run!>

The tentacles undulate, thorned tips moving in unison. They reach for me, yearning for contact. Mournful green eyes and brown eyes stare about between them.

The cat hisses at me, thorn teeth shining silver. Her fur shimmers through a muted rainbow as her size grows from house cat to tiger.

<Allison! Run!>

The cat gives one last electric flicker and becomes something fully solid. Bronze metal quills replace soft fur. Her tail swishes, fanning me with moss-musty wind laced with bone dust.

My arm pulses and screams agony in time with her swishing.

A foul taste sits in my mouth. Coppery. I can't tell if it's from my lungs or from the fetid odor now rising from my arm.

The tentacles reach, thorns transforming into soft tips. They look gentle, far more gentle than the cat.

<Allison>

Something shines in the transient sunlight beyond the cat, beyond the end of the tunnel. My eyes relax as I struggle to focus on the object. Flag stickers and some numbers. *Must be the cargo drop.* Not intended for us, but instead for the scientists who vanished without even sending a distress call. Without finishing the blood-soaked meals on their tables.

If I can get around the cat, I can reach it. So close. A quick dash, then there.

Hot. So hot. Cold to hot, no in-between, frozen inferno. This fever...

I struggle out of my overshirt and drop it onto the moss. It lands with a squish. The moss snorts like a team of tiny horses and absorbs the shirt halfway. I don't want it back.

It smells like death, anyway.

Sweat runs down my back, further soaking my filthy undershirt. It pools above what's left of my belt.

Clothes in tatters—*how long have I been here? An hour? Ten years?* The cat watches me as I try to decipher my memories.

I remember running. I remember snagging my arm on the vine while the crew screamed. Muscles tearing, bones crunching, screaming. Before that, the snap-splinter of Tilly's bones and her screams as a thing dragged her away.

What thing? Why can't I remember? There were tentacles then, too. But what else? Eyes?

The cat blinks at me and bares her thorn teeth. Bone splinters and sinew are caught between them.

<Allison. Allison, run. Run to me, Allison, to me!>

The cat lets out a rumbling purr. I spin around to face the direction I started from. Something moves in the gray light. Tentacles dangle like living curtains, blocking the view.

My head hurts so much, from eyes to nape. I spit blood and mucus onto the remnants of my overshirt and try to focus my vision between tentacle ripples.

"Allison. I love you, Allison." The whisper condenses to one solid location.

Tilly's freckled hand pushes the tentacles aside. She's dirty and bruised, but her eyes—green left, brown right—shine like stars in the familiar comfort of her face.

Her form flickers. She smiles and holds out a hand. "You're going the wrong way, love."

"I'm going to the cargo drop. I need medicine."

She tilts her head, shrugs. "You can go to the crate, but for what? The portal has closed. If you save yourself, you will spend the rest of your life utterly and completely alone. Isolated, insignificant, meaningless."

A shiver rises, chill blanketing heat. "You aren't real."

Tilly laughs. "I am real. I'm here, aren't I?"

"Your eyes are backward."

Tilly looks down. She flickers and shimmers, then looks up. Her odd eyes are on their correct sides. "Mirrors are our image memories of ourselves, love. We can never see ourselves as others do, only remember the mirror direction." She extends her arm again. Hand bones rise from the moss just an inch or two, then settle back with a creak and groan.

"I want a med pack." Why does my arm hurt so much? I could tolerate it until now because the ribs were worse, but this is nerve fire and a thousand acid needles.

"What's the point?" Tilly retracts her hand. She rubs the bridge of her nose and clicks her tongue, typical Tilly style. "You sent that warning signal through the gate, Allison. You closed the portal. No one will come here now. No one can. No one to learn, no one to play. No one to nurture. You're going to die here, love. Your choice—running on and fighting alone for nothing, or here with me. With me, part of me, part of each other like we've always been."

"You're not Tilly. My Tilly would never tell me to give up." My legs go numb and I slip to the ground. I'm so tired, so tired. It's hard to move. Maybe if I can move, if I can convince my legs to work. Maybe I can make it to the crate.

Tilly crouches in front of me. Her red and yellow polka-dot socks bring whimsy to the gray. She touches her forehead to mine and rubs the back of my neck with one hand. Her fingertips, warm and dry, release a small muscle knot, relieving a pain I'd ignored. She kisses my lips. Tastes like strawberries. The chemical kind, not the real. She has used the same flavor lip balm since before our beginning.

She shakes her head and sighs. "Not giving up. Giving in. Becoming, not ending. This world is alive and I'm part of it now, forever. I want you to be, too. I love you so much and I want to keep you with me. I don't want to lose you. I don't want this pain for you. Let's stop the pain."

I'm too tired to speak. Legs are lead, vision is as much a tunnel as the one I'm in.

Eyes blink from the walls, skeletal fingers reach from the moss. Tentacles reaching, tentacles writhing. The cat circles, small again, approving.

This is wrong, all wrong. No one can help me. I'm alone here, on this planet. Maybe in this galaxy.

"Get away from me!" I scream, startling Tilly. *I'm not ready to die. I don't want to.*

"Part of me forever, love, part of everything beautiful and alive. You will finally have meaning. You'll feel different soon. I promise. No pain or fear. It's wonderful, you'll see."

I can't move. *Why can't I move?* I try to protest, but only one word moves past my cracked lips. "Shit."

Tilly wipes blood and mud from my face. She studies it, sniffs it, licks it from her fingertips. I can barely see, except for her face and the ribs full of heart, beating frantically in anticipation as the tentacles descend, tipped with retractable claws, moss reaching, pain shrieking teeth between eyes of brown and green cold so cold can't move can't fight can't scream—

Can't breathe—

Can't breathe—

Can't—

<Allison. I love you, my sweet Allison. Just a caress now, just a lover's touch, venom and teeth. No pain, no fear, just two heartbeats and sleep.>

Eulogy of an Empty Stargate

By Rosalind Weir

Don't make a sound.

You caught a glimpse of their bodies on the floor, didn't you? Of course. Well, so long as you're good for me, there's no need to end up down there with them. There's no need to see them either. See? I've got your eyes. That's got to be some comfort for you. You can stay safe and sound within your own little head, and I'll stay out here, watching as they writhe in the dark red light, their ribs caving in on themselves as they gasp for breath in a hot wet death throe. You probably couldn't even make out the blood pooling beneath their bodies before I crept in through your ears. No? Good.

What's your name? Come, come. You can speak. Just do what I ask, and everything will be fine.

"J-Jason."

That's hilarious. Jason and the Argonauts. I'll bet you're the captain of this fine vessel. Hm?

"No. I-I'm the navigator."

Practically the captain, then. How many star systems have you explored, then? Hundreds? Thousands? Or is this your first or second? You look pretty young, although I know technology has grown in its infinite capabilities. For all I know, you could be in your hundreds and still appear to be barely shy of twenty. And you have quite the good body too, Jason. That poor girl over there, Amelia. She was good like you, but between the quiet cancerous cells rippling through her bones and her useless job as a clerk, well… you can see why I couldn't occupy her now. In a way, it's almost a mercy that she's going like this. You humans never could quite figure out the cancer thing. Unless I'm mistaken?

"No."

No. I thought as much.

Well, Jason, for today, we're going to be very good friends. Now that you've introduced yourself, I'm going to introduce myself, and then you're going to do exactly what I tell you. And then I'll leave forever. I won't bother you again. If I'm feeling nice, I may even give you back your sight. That's fair, right? Right?

I don't like to be ignored, Jason.

"Right. Sorry. You're right."

"Sorry?" I think I'm definitely going to like you. Some of these little bastards could learn some manners. Like your chief medical officer. What was his name? Lane? Lane. I suppose I'm lucky that physicians aren't allowed to carry guns. He tried to steal one from the general and blast me out of his brain. Not that the general's reaction was much better when I jumped to him. But I'm sure you don't want to hear much about that. You don't seem like the sort of person who would enjoy hearing about the deaths of each and every one of his crewmates. Unless you're a little bit of a sadist?

I'll take that as a no.

Let's sit down. Take a step to your right. Now another. Reach your hand out in front of you. Do you feel the top of the chair? I feel it with you, cold despite the blazing heater rushing through this place. I'd ask you to turn it off, but then again, that might be a bit too much work for you in this state. Now, turn it around and sit down. Nice and easy. See? That wasn't so hard. Oh, and ignore that twitching near your ankle. Believe me, you don't want to know what's become of that poor old lady. Make sure that you don't look down when I give you your sight back. I'm not sure if you'll remember that piece of advice by the time we're through, but don't say I didn't warn you.

Are you comfortable?

"Why do you care?"

I just thought you should sit down for this. I'd hate for you to faint and ruin that pretty little head of yours. That got your friend Miron. He was so good for me. At the very least, he tried. He just couldn't handle it, though. He began shaking, like a thousand little earthquakes had been sparked in his nerves, and his legs collapsed out from underneath him. He hit his head on the control panel. I feel his life ebbing away. He's still alive, but at that moment, I feared that he might slip from this world and take me with him. I barely escaped into a bridge crewman before that happened. I'm sure that it's no consolation that his last thoughts were of you.

He truly loved you. If you help me quickly, you might still be able to save your best friend.

"Please..."

You want that, don't you? He's the only thing you have left.

"Just... let me save him... let me live, and let me save him. I'll do whatever you want."

I knew I finally made the right decision.

I suppose you want to know what I am then.

This universe was born out of a quantum fluctuation in a false vacuum. Multiple universes have formed in this way. Your universe is not unique, neither the first nor the last, but like a card in a game of blackjack, your universe is a random one, generated from an amalgamation of borrowed energy and particles that lived slightly longer than fate ordained that they should have. My universe is a similar one that formed in such a way that it became positioned nearby yours. Perhaps it was because ours were born around the same time—cosmic fraternal twins of sorts—or perhaps it's for some other reason unknown to neither man nor monster.

Your universe evolved from its own Big Bang, and so did mine. But in mine, everything was oh so different. There was no light in the universe, just masses of heat and masses of cold floating in an empty void that varied in consistency and composition. Some of these masses were lighter than air, so clear that you could float through them, and some were so dense that they collapsed into a dimension that cannot be perceived. The most impressive spots, however, were the stargates, rips through our dimensions, windows to other worlds. There was an infinite space filled with these spots— the light, the dense, and the portals—and everything was completely silent.

It was absolutely perfect.

From this nothingness came my race. We formed out of the cold space and were enveloped in the warmth. We desired warmth. We occupied it. We were even more elusive than the depths of empty space, so we wormed our way into the warm blocks of heaviness that floated in the nothingness, and we hibernated. Soon, however, we desired much more. We wanted knowledge. We wanted to have connections with each other. We wanted to feed. So, we did what felt natural. We began to go through the stargates.

I can see your mind churning, your thoughts flicking by me so quickly that I fear they may knock me on my back. We were practically nothing. We were the only things that could freely travel in and out of the stargates to this world without being trapped within them, without being trapped within the black holes—the remnants of stars that died so spectacularly that they tore through the fabric of space. We made it to your Einstein-Rosen bridges and gathered just enough strength to prop them open as we traveled between the worlds. We saw the most beautiful things as we did so, but to me, none were as beautiful as this world.

I came back here time and time again to soak in the knowledge of this place. I watched disks of gas and dust birth stars and planetary systems that shone with such ferocity that I was nearly blinded. I watched spiral galaxies in the beginning stages of the universe collide to form ellipticals, appreciating every single moment of the train wreck as time passed around me. I watched the deaths of stars, and then the deaths of their progyny, as the white dwarfs slowly faded to black, and the blazing neutron stars lost their beaming energy, as your own black holes eventually fizzled out. It all felt so slow, like swimming in honey, but it was sweet nonetheless.

I watched civilizations emerge from oceans, then fizzle out and die all the same. There should have been millions in your universe alone, but you just kept destroying yourselves until, at last, only one could survive at a time. It's hard enough for life to form at first. One species in billions rises to extreme heights on one planet, only to be snuffed out by nuclear weapons, by neglect of the planet, by your own greed and selfishness. It was so horrific to me, but so comforting to know that could never happen to us. We are timeless. We are eternal. We will never destroy each other.

I eventually realized that I was emerging in this place at different times. Time works differently around black holes. I witnessed the death of this universe before I witnessed its birth. I witnessed humanity's destruction before

Earth even formed. I sought to find the perfect time, the most exciting knowledge to steal for myself, to keep in my own mind ike a pirate's treasure and preside over for the rest of eternity.

The more knowledge I accumulate, however, the heavier I become. Each time I traveled to my own universe, it became much more difficult to emerge. The last time I tried, I became trapped here. I was too heavy to fit through the bridge and too weak to hold it open, and it collapsed on me as I tried to squeeze through. I lost half of myself, just how black holes themselves eventually dissipate, and the conscious part of me that survived was left stuck here.

I've been calling out for help ever since. I just want to go home. I'm so tired of this world. This was meant to be my last visit here, but something went horribly wrong, and now I'm trapped. I don't want to be here anymore. I've finished devouring information, consuming the knowledge that permeates your world. I want to sleep now. I want to crawl into a hot dense gas, and fall into a deep slumber from which I will never awaken.

You can understand why I want that, don't you?

You want that to happen to me, too. You want me to leave you alone, right?

"Y-Yes..."

I know everything. All you need to do is follow my directions. Everything will be as it should.

"How...? How do we begin?"

That's the fun part. I'm sure your chief of science officer wou d have known all about it, but alas, she wasn't in this room when I came aboard your vessel, and I wanted to limit myself. There's no sense in causing a panic, is there? That would make my work so much harder. That's all right, though. I extracted as much information as possible from the mind of the little engineer. Somewhere on this ship, there is an antigravity contraption and a miniature vessel, barely large enough to comfortably fit a dog. As your ship traveled close to M51, they were going to release the machine into the black hole. They created signals that would rip small holes between our universe—barely enough to notice, like stitches in a dress—so that it would let them know when it passed through the Einstein-Rosen bridge. I found you before they could deploy it, however.

I'd like to do that experiment, but with a modification. Instead of passing a small object through the bridge, however, I would like tc extend the machine's effects to the whole ship. That way, we can both ensure that I'll reach the other side. That way, you also won't let anything go wrong. If you try to betray me, we'll send you, your little friend, and everyone else on this ship to their doom. You'll all be spaghettified, and I'll escape to try again with a different, much smarter, group. But I don't think that will happen. I think you're perfectly competent. So, when our plan works, we'll come out the other side in my universe. You'll be able to turn right back around and leave after you ensure I get to where I need to be. Then we can both go about our own lives.

Do we have a deal?

Jason.

I could hurt you so easily right now. I could slip my fingers into your synapses. All it would take is for me to jolt, and your mind will be destroyed. It wouldn't kill you, though. I'd slip into your bloodstream and travel deep into your heart. I'd destroy it with clotting, and then leave to stab through the rest of your limbs, your organs, your cells, and your very particles. You would be in such excruciating agony that by the time I left, you wouldn't even be able to sense that you've regained your sight past the searing red. You wouldn't be able to see the face of your best friend, inches away from your own, as your body slowly broke down on you. And then, you'd disappear, and I'd just try someone else, as many times as it takes, until I find someone who will listen. There are children somewhere on this ship. I'm sure one is smart enough to obey me.

"You'll... you'll leave us alone... if I do this. Right...? Right?"

I will. I promise.

The first thing you need to do is give up control.

It's almost too easy to move your body, Jason.

I wonder if you're like me right now, if you can sense what I'm saying and doing with your limbs, or if you're just floating around your own mind. Perhaps you're sitting deep within yourself, screaming for help until I summon your thoughts and memories. I feel a wave of terror whenever I pull for your help to navigate this ship, to attach the antigravity device, to steer the ship toward its final destination.

It feels almost pleasant when the ship is pulled into the ginormous embrace of the darkness. I feel so much more than the rest of you, the humans who don't realize that anything is amiss until they see the event horizon approaching. For you, there is a heaviness. Your body wants to fall to the ground, but it is only propped upright by myself. For you, there is a tugging sensation that threatens to rip your body apart, down to your molecules, and then some. Don't worry, though. This black hole is much too large for that to truly happen. Most of you will get through in one piece. For me, though, there is an ethereal weightlessness as I enter my warm home, slick with the heat of all the bodies worming their way back inside after our feeding, filled with the breath of knowledge as my species slowly settles in for their slumber.

Isn't it lovely? And here I thought your universe was the most beautiful thing in the world. But no. I am. We are. We are the beginning and end of everything. We are the destruction of the final thing left in the world, even after all the stars explode and fade, after all of the planets crumble, after black holes dissipate in the sweetness of quantum tunneling. We are truly all there is, the atoms and the void, the dividing line between life and death.

We are the devourers of worlds. We ended yours, deep in the future.

I think we were the beginning of the end for all possible universes. All that is, all that there ever will be, and all that there ever was, dies with our existence.

We're here.

You should heed my advice for one last time. You should try to leave as soon as possible. As far as I know, your ship and its inhabitants are the only things made of knowledge in this world. While my brethren have already had their fill, there are some things out there that are much more dangerous than us. Some of them didn't make it through the stargate. Some of them are still ravenous. They already have their eyes on you.

Be careful. They're getting close to you.

Goodbye.

Il Virgo Idolin

by Lou Kemp

Kinsky had held the fish, its jaws working spasmodically and gulping air. The knife reflected sunlight as it flashed across its belly, spilling blood and entrails. Kinsky brought the knife down, severing the head. On other ships and on other excursions, Helen had watched fish gutted. Every time the head is cut off first, as a form of mercy. Not now.

"Here, you bastards!" He flung a handful of bloody guts into the air.

From the army of birds following the ship, a gull swooped, catching the fish head before it disappeared into the foaming waves trailing the ship.

Kinsky slapped another fish onto the cutting board and a fine spray flecked her arm and dress.

"Sorry, Miss." Kinsky grinned. His one gold tooth and a few wooden ones made him appear comical—until his feral, empty eyes met hers. She turned away before he could see the gnawing fear in her own.

The ship rode high waves and wind that snapped the sails taunt and tugged at the parasol in her hand. To the east, a bank of clouds crowded the horizon. Glistening like millions of reflected diamonds, the sea seemed endless as it disappeared into the horizon.

"Too bad about the Rev'rend." With his muscles straining, he heaved a barrel onto the upper deck. Helen wrinkled her nose. Above the smell of fish, his odor fouled the air. When she did not respond, Kinsky spoke louder.

"Isn't it a bleeding shame, Miss?"

She hadn't forgotten.

On the night he vanished, the reverend had regaled fellow passengers with talk of Philadelphia, the Indian War just ended, and the ungodly wild land of Alaska. Around his neck, a bible dangled from a silk cord—for ease of reading scripture to those in need of salvation. Long after the moon climbed high, the reverend and Jim argued over slavery and rights. Fatigue and the ship swaying in a gentle rhythm finally drove Helen to her cabin.

Under a steaming sun the next morning, Helen watched as the crew searched the ship. Something did not feel right. And when she saw Kinsky leering from the background, wearing the same smile he used to gut fish, she felt a sense of dread stirring that wouldn't go away. The captain announced that the reverend must have fallen overboard during the night.

At first, Helen had believed him. She had no reason not to. But when she had found the torn cord from the reverend's bible between the bulkheads, the finger of unease returned to wiggle slowly down her back. There it lingered and grew under a blazing sun.

A deckhand shouted as the boom creaked and swung around. As the wind shifted to the south, Helen ducked and retreated to the stern, lifting her face into the dying sun and cool spray from the sea. Only a week north of San Francisco and the days already grew colder and shorter.

A hand circled her waist. She screamed and swung her parasol.

"Helen—" Jim said, his arms enveloping her.

She relaxed against him, breathing again. The feminine weapon fell from her hands.

"Who did you think it was?" Jim murmured into her hair.

"I don't know." *Any one of the hungry-eyed sailors, or Kinsky*, she thought.

"You've been nervous since we boarded the ship." Jim took her hand. "Come inside. The captain would like to toast our betrothal." He led her across the deck to the salon, stooping under the low doorway and into opulence.

Velvet drapes, rich wood, and the warmth a well-stocked bar induced made the salon their social center for the new few weeks. A monstrous and beautiful pipe organ took up an entire wall facing the stern. Leaded windows on both sides framed a picture of the sunset. Helen felt like she stood in a plush cave. Or womb. A lamp burned low upon the bar that spanned the leeward side of the room. From a shadowy corner, labored breathing reached her ears.

"Mrs. Wiggins?" Slipping from Jim's arms, Helen groped for a candle beside the door and lit it as she approached one of the sofas.

Tiny and delicate before boarding The Prudence, Mrs. Wiggins had shriveled under an unknown illness. Wan eyes blinked against the candlelight and the elderly woman's forehead felt cool, almost cold. Helen sat beside her and tried to smile.

"Why aren't you resting in your cabin, Mrs. Wiggins?" Jim asked as he went about the room lighting lamps.

"Captain Godfrey kindly carried me here," Mrs. Wiggins replied. She had succumbed to the captain's charm. Unlike Jim.

"And left you alone in the dark?"

"No." It cost Mrs. Wiggins to speak. "The draft blew out the light." She pointed to a high shelf and burned-out candles.

Helen had felt the drafts, too, finding no gaps in the fine paneling, yet feeling the chill of icy fingers that played a soft staccato down her neck.

"Well." Jim could sound like a stuffed shirt. "Captain God shouldn't have left you."

"Jim!" Helen exclaimed.

He waved it away and changed the subject. "Anyhow, he says The Prudence used to carry a different cargo than what he has stowed below."

Only weeks ago, Helen had said her farewells on the dock and watched barrels of whiskey loaded into the hold. The ship would pick up pine and redwood when it docked in Vancouver. She too had heard the old stories that circulated around San Francisco; years ago, ships captained by pirates kidnapped round-eyed fair women and sold them in the Orient. She knew that was a thing of the past.

Like someone had opened an undersea floodgate, the sea shifted, and the ship descended suddenly into a trough between waves. The Prudence crested high and came down hard, bottoming out before plowing forward again. Mrs. Wiggins's color faded, and Helen graspec for her hand.

The starboard door opened. As the captain strode into the room, Helen watched Jim stiffen. She compared them, noting their eyes could meet on the same level. But there the similarity ended. Fair and temperate, Jim warmed the room like the sun. The captain's charms brooded, handsome and arrogant, hair black as the night.

"Good evening, Miss Carpenter, Mr. Lewis," Captain Godfrey addressed them with a bow before he crossed over to stand in front of Mrs. Wiggins.

With his erect posture and military bearing, the captain could have appeared as an escort at a royal wedding. As he dropped to one knee, he kissed the old woman's hand. "How do you feel, Mrs. Wiggins?"

Helen's attention strayed beyond him to the dying sun as it bled through the windows, reflecting like blood on the brass pipes of the organ. The pipes ascended by degrees to embrace the ceiling. Even from a distance, the ivory keys and the intricate carving of the polished mahogany of the organ caught her eye. In the rainbow of light, the carved figures seemed alive.

"I'm a mite tired, Captain," Mrs. Wiggins answered. Helen winced at the weakness in her voice.

"A bit of champagne will make you feel better," the captain announced and moved to the bar.

Jim stood over Mrs. Wiggins, frowning, and sharing Helen's fears for her health. The captain handed them glasses.

"To the betrothal of Helen Jane Carpenter and James Daniel Lewis."

They touched glasses. As the sweet-sour bubbles tickled Helen's nose, she wondered why their full names should be on the tip of the captain's tongue. Although she avoided his direct, accessing gaze, she could still feel it.

"Miss Carpenter, may I ask why you are traveling to Fairbanks?" Captain Godfrey poured more champagne.

"My father awaits us. The wedding will take place at the settlement next spring."

Captain Godfrey said, "Your father is the wealthiest man in the Territories."

Jim reddened.

"What does that—"

"You are marrying a wealthy woman." Captain Godfrey sounded as courteous and bland as if he'd been asked to describe a bank transaction. "And a beautiful one."

Jim's arm around her shoulder tightened and his chin came up. "I love Helen."

The captain's expression was enigmatic as he turned away to the champagne bottle. "Of course."

Helen sat with Mrs. Wiggins through the evening as she pecked at her dinner and tried to shoo her away. The ailing woman had been employed as her companion, but Helen felt she was hers instead. When her friend finally slept, Helen drew on a wrap and sought fresh air.

From the crew's quarters floated sounds of card playing and voices in many languages. An empty bottle sailed over the rail and landed with a splash into a calm sea.

When Helen shut the salon door behind her, she gestured for Jim and the captain to be seated. It appeared that they had declared peace under the hazy smoke of cigars and more champagne.

"Has the ship always been called The Prudence, Captain?" Jim asked, taking Helen's hand and pulling her down to the sofa beside him.

He clipped his answer. "No, it has not."

"What was she called?" Jim persisted.

The captain poured a third glass that he handed to Helen. "*il Idolin.*"

"What does that mean?" Jim asked.

"I'm sure I do not know." Captain Godfrey shrugged, turning to address Helen. "Your fiancée reports you are an accomplished musician, Miss Carpenter."

"She has given concerts at the Opera Hall," Jim said.

"Excellent!" the captain exclaimed. "Please honor us." He swept a hand toward the organ. "A Wasserman from Munich."

Since boarding The Prudence, Helen had resisted playing the instrument, delaying the pleasure so that it would not grow stale during the long voyage. As she walked to the other side of the salon, the murmurs from Jim and the captain that followed her from across the room seemed to dim. For a moment, she stood before the beautiful instrument: secretly, she had always thought that fine instruments were as alive as she, and each had a separate and distinct personality. Why else would they need to be tuned constantly, and most delicately?

With care, she caressed the intricate carving of devil-like creatures leaping amid sealife. From under her lashes, she studied the captain. "*il Idolin*" he had said. She would think the captain *did* know Latin. Perhaps he was superstitious.

When she sat before the organ, her curiosity faded as she touched a key. And another.

The notes evolved to melodies, the tone rich and pure. She played from memory, forgetting the uneasiness she'd known since boarding the ship, letting thoughts of the captain flood her senses as the music turned melancholy. As her hands flew up the scales, she closed her eyes and again stood on stage hearing applause like the sound of thousands of blackbirds beating their wings against the darkness. Helen pumped the pedals, and the pipes rang, reverberating and spilling rich music into the night.

As the crescendo built, the room grew cold, and the drafts returned. The indistinct shadows in the air seemed to move faster.

In the aftermath of the music, Helen felt Jim standing behind her. The captain stayed to the side. She met his eye, seeing more of him tonight than in the week they had been sailing.

Helen asked, "Does my music please you, Captain?" Her fingers danced an ascending minor scale toward him, the sound like a woman's mystery, full and enticing.

He nodded; his expression hooded.

"It is said that music is pure emotion." Under her hand, the notes descended toward Jim in a clear major key, the sound honest and clean. Moralistic. She ran an intricate race in a series of notes from the lower minor keys, zigzagging up the scale toward the captain. "Played with control, it is civilized, and accepted."

"It is a choice," Captain Godfrey replied, and lifted his glass to drink. His eyes bored into hers. "We do what we must do."

Helen's brows drew together. Such a strange reply. The captain opened the door leading to the starboard deck and gazed beyond The Prudence's lights, into the black void of the sea. She instinctively knew he still listened. Helen allowed her musings to dissolve into the music, playing without direction, sensations stirring around the room that she could feel with her eyes closed.

Five notes. She repeated them because they entered unbidden into her thoughts. With them came the drafts that chilled the air and raced about the salon, extinguishing the candles on top of the organ with a swift, invisible hand.

Hours later, she tried to sleep, but the notes repeated in her mind. Helen writhed in the covers of her bunk as the music grew louder, seeming to come from everywhere to fill the cabin. Long into the night, Mrs. Wiggins's labored breathing rose and fell, keeping time with the waves as they rocked the hull of The Prudence.

In an infant dawn, Helen awoke, bathed in the weak sunlight filtering through the porthole. A glance through the gloom of the cabin revealed that Mrs. Wiggins lay still. Helen dressed quietly, brushed her hair, and prepared to go on deck. At the door, she paused.

The labored breathing had died during the night.

All day Helen stood at the bow, a forlorn masthead, grieving. For a long time, she couldn't face her loss as she gazed into the rushing waves. With a sob, she leaned into Jim's embrace. And warmth. As she listened to his heartbeat, she wasn't sure if she could live and lose him, too.

When the day became twilight, they met the captain for dinner in the salon. The occasion rang empty, the quiet a reminder of how during the first week at sea before his death, the reverend had toasted glasses with Mrs. Wiggins and engaged in spirited conversations. Helen left the men to their brandies, gazing out the door to inhale the night. The breeze freshened, lifting her hair and letting it fall again as the Prudence drifted in the current, the water too deep to anchor.

From the salon, Jim's murmur came, then his laughter. His tolerance of the captain had grown over the last few days. While he saw nothing sinister in this second death, she felt a malignancy. Waiting.

By dawn the sea tossed The Prudence with a rough hand, the clouds background to a growing squall.

In the skies, unseen giants filled their cheeks, billowing the seas. While the wind howled and the sea rose and fell, inside their room Helen packed Mrs. Higgins's possessions with a heavy heart.

Midday descended into an eerie darkness, broken by jagged streaks of lightning. As rain beat on the roof of the cabin with incessant fingers, Helen shrugged; she had ridden out storms before. Pressing her face to the glass, she saw only a sweeping mist through which a crewman sometimes ran.

For the rest of the day and the next, Helen remained secluded in her cabin. Occasionally, she'd peek out her door, seeing the decks remained wet and the gales still strong. The captain sent his apologies for her confinement; The Prudence could not spare a sailor to keep her from blowing over the side.

Jim had knocked once around midnight, bellowing a drunken good night.

Helen awoke ravenous. Wrapped in her warmest cape, she struggled to open the rain-swollen cabin door, and when she did, a blast of icy rain stung her face as she skidded across the shifting deck to grab the rail.

Helen knocked on Jim's door. Then again, louder.

"Jim!" No response. Helen opened the door.

Weak light revealed a bunk not slept in. Helen took a deep breath. She wanted to believe he could have slept in the salon. Perhaps he and the captain had been dipping into the brandy again, keeping the storm company. As she staggered across the deck, The Prudence picked up more wind, beginning to climb the waves.

The salon lay in darkness, curtains drawn, trapping the smell of stale cigars and drink. Faintly, almost too softly to hear, the five notes returned. Her unease began to bleed, and she ran outside.

A deckhand went by, affecting the swaggered walk peculiar to all sailors. Helen intercepted him. "Please, Mr. Lewis? Where is he?" The sailor grunted and pointed to the bridge.

Helen looked upward. The bridge was accessed by a rain-slicked ladder and the wind blew her cape back as she climbed, and her skirts flew until she fluttered like a bird on the rail.

The captain frowned as he spun the wheel starboard. Helen yelled above the noise of the ship.

"Have you seen Mr. Lewis?"

The captain scowled and gestured for Kinsky to take the wheel.

"Women do not belong on the bridge." He took her arm and led her to the side. "Come."

He descended the first few steps and then dangled her over the deck and onto her feet before swinging down beside her.

"Captain!"

"Please excuse the familiarity, Miss Carpenter." He did not smi e. "But a woman aboard ship has always been unlucky; one on the bridge can only mean disaster."

With his words, a cold sun broke through the dissipating cloucs. How alien she felt on a ship of men.

"I cannot find Jim."

The captain rubbed his chin. "His cabin?"

She shook her head. "Nor the salon."

"He must be about." The captain shrugged and said, "Perhaps Mr. Lewis is in the galley."

The five notes nudged her with cold fingers. She looked up.

Kinsky leaned over the rail of the bridge, eyes glittering in the new sun. She recognized the same morbid happiness that had swam in his eyes twice before with the butchering of the fish and the disappearance of the reverend.

A hum of voices reached them. Helen pushed beyond the captain and looked to the bow. In front of the storage lockers, a quartet of sailors backed toward the rail carrying a shrouded bundle. They lifted it high.

"JIM!" Helen screamed and ran forward.

Kinsky caught her with bruising hands. The captain gestured and the sailors heaved the bundle over the side. Helen screamed again and the music whispered. The tarp binding the bundle unfurled in the wind as it fell. When it hit the water, the image of a pale face and bloodstained shirt faded as the waves swallowed the body.

She broke away from Kinsky's grip.

"Oh, Jim," she whispered to the waves as they rose and fell, the surface unbroken by death.

In the silence, the sailors and Captain Godfrey waited behind her; party to murder. With a cry, she faced them. The spray from the leaping waves soaked her back.

The captain gestured impatiently and sent the sailors back to work. Kinsky remained at his side, grinning like a faithful rabid dog.

"Your fiancée met with an unfortunate accident. We wished to spare your sensibilities," the captain said.

"He was murdered!" Helen cried.

"I am the law on this ship, Miss Carpenter. You would do well to remember that." The captain's gaze locked with hers. "Mr. Lewis slipped and hit his head. He died this morning."

"No—" Her voice rose.

"Go back to your cabin. Compose yourself." He no longer pretended compassion. "Mr. Lewis had a regrettable accident. Upon reflection, you will agree."

Helen shuddered from her fingers to her toes. Kinsky stepped closer.

"Take her away."

As The Prudence sailed north, the air blew colder and land masses under snow-capped peaks ringed the eastern horizon. Helen knew they would not stop in Vancouver, the declaration to pick up more cargo had been a blind. Would they dock at a forgotten outpost to pick up more contraband? Could she escape then?

The days evolved into a pattern as Helen wrapped herself in isolation and grief for Jim, Mrs. Wiggins, and the reverend. She feared everyone aboard The Prudence. Especially Kinsky.

A week passed since Helen had spoken to anyone and the day she saw Jim's frozen face slip beneath the waves. This evening, she crept into the salon to stand before the opaque windows and the loneliness she felt settled deeper into her bones.

The organ sat in the shadows, mirroring her despair. She knew comfort could be found in talk, in whiskey, in random acts of self-destruction. Her own came from music, and to touch the keys meant solace.

She placed a candelabra upon the organ, steadying it as the ship rocked in the current. For a long time, she sat before the instrument, not touching the keys or pedals. The cold drafts, like sprites in the night, whirled around the room. Waiting. As the candlelight flickered, it danced on the pipes, firing the metal, and bringing the carved figures to life. In the corner of her mind, the five elusive notes returned.

Ignoring them, she began a funeral march. Slow, ponderous, and melancholy, the music wallowed in the atmosphere of gloom.

Dimly, the sound came of the leeward door opening. Then a callused and fishy hand covered her mouth. She screamed as an arm lifted her up and around.

Kinsky squeezed her into his chest. She bit his hand, and her scream filled the air. The emptiness in his eyes propelled her feet as she kicked and struggled. He laughed and ripped her dress, pulling her head back with a handful of hair. She screamed again. Cold air flooded the room, and he dropped her.

The captain backhanded Kinsky, sending him spinning across the room, knocking over a table. An oil lamp fell as flames raced up the velvet curtains.

Kinsky tore the curtain down, rolling it into a ball and smothering the fire.

Holding her dress closed, Helen stood.

"Hands off—" The cold menace in Captain Godfrey's voice cut. "We deliver undamaged goods."

Kinsky wiped blood from his chin and spat a wooden tooth. His hate-filled eyes fell upon her. Helen ducked behind the captain.

"Hide, little virgin!" Kinsky shoved a chair aside and headed for the door. "I want me money more!" He slammed the door, rattling the bottles above the bar.

"What does he mean?" she whispered.

Captain Godfrey turned, his face partly in shadow. "Your father is a rich man. When we reach Hong Kong, he will pay handsomely for you." He gripped her chin. "I have a buyer for beautiful flesh who will pay even more."

He caught her raised hand and pulled her closer.

"I keep Kinsky away for another reason." His knee imprisoned Helen against the organ. As he tried to kiss her, she twisted away.

"Witnesses are easy to be rid of," Captain Godfrey said. "A little poison for the old lady and a shove off the side for the preacher." His finger traced the hollow at her neck.

"No!"

"I'll have you before we reach the China Sea." He pushed her toward the door. "Go!"

Three more days and the ship entered the sea west of the Aleutian Islands. The weather worsened with Helen's spirits; the blood of three people stained her hands. Could she blow the ship to Hell she would do so.

All afternoon, she'd heard fear in the whispered conversations of the crew. Barometer readings warned of a fierce and powerful storm ahead. From concealment in a storage bay, Helen listened to the captain discuss emergency procedures with Kinsky. Instead of obeying maritime broadcasts requesting all ships to head south or put into port, they continued on course northward. With his contraband, Captain Godfrey intended to ride the storm out.

The winds lessened over the next few hours, and she felt the air grow colder as the ship slowed under the rain. She stood alone in the shadow of the bulkheads. The rain turned to snow that stuck to her eyelashes and floated in bright drifts on the water. Like the crew, Helen began to see shapes in the water and submerged ice that preyed on her nerves. To the north, everything was painted white.

Midnight. With long iron poles, the crew patrolled the decks, ready to push the ship free from ice floes.

In the distance, the roar of a sea lion rumbled, the sound riding the growing wind as they drifted into the monstrous storm. Helen ran for her cabin as the rain became a deluge, as if a celestial bucket upended upon them. In minutes, the storm devoured the ship, with the waves and rain increasing ten-fold.

The Prudence suddenly shifted. From deep below, a mortal groan shuddered the ship's timbers. Like a chorus of banshees, the wind shrieked through the yardarms, treating the canvasses like tissue paper, and roaring to the heavens again. When the five notes began, Helen was not surprised; it seemed so appropriate.

The blizzard turned night into day. Soft mounds of snow floated like dumplings in a broth of black water. Between them, Helen thought she saw Jim, his mouth open, calling her name.

Without warning, the wind tumbled her to the deck, and like a doll, she rolled the length of the ship. She crawled across nets and puddles of greasy water to the salon. On the fringes of her mind, the five notes tarried, discordant and insistent. As she watched, a wave of slush and seawater broke over the leeward side, sweeping one of the sailors overboard.

Ascending and descending, five notes in A minor, playing the internal shadows of her mind. With bare hands, she battled to open the salon door. Helen heard a rumbling from the stern and turned.

Riding a great roar of wind above the ship, a wall of snow blew toward The Prudence. Helen wrenched the door open and fell into the darkened room as the door slammed shut behind her. Before she could decide what to do, The Prudence shuddered and slid through the ice, turning 180 degrees, swinging to starboard.

Helen staggered to the foot of the organ. Over the wind, she heard the shouting of the sailors as the ship pitched onto its side. She fell into the wall and then to the floor. On deck, the commands of Captain Godfrey thundered, competing with the gales. Through the curtainless window, she saw Kinsky run by, his eyes wide and his fear unholy.

More shouts came from the captain, and the ship righted itself. The fury of the storm increased with an awful tearing of wood. Then, with a shudder that shook the timbers, the ship began to *move*.

Music, only music, she whispered. Helen pulled herself up by the pipes, to sit before the keys.

As the five notes reverberated, the sound pulsed repeating, and becoming painful. Helen covered her ears and still the music played. Then the notes quieted to a compelling and beseeching murmur as if the music whispered to her, imploring, like a discarded child. The carving of the sea nymphs and devils blurred before her and then came alive in the white light of the swirling snow.

The notes flowed slowly from her hands. Carefully, she repeated them, building them into an ancient rhythm that could no longer be ignored. She stomped on the bellows, until the music rang in the frigid air, bleating above the fury of the storm and cries of the doomed sailors.

The cadence became electric, marching forward as the storm grew still fiercer, propelling the ship with a ghostly hand, lifting the vessel out of the water, and dropping it again. Damned, The Prudence picked up incredible speed, racing into a frozen void.

The drafts in the salon, released at last, blew cold, reveling in the music. As the music grew louder than the storm, Helen gripped the sides of the organ.

The Prudence shuddered and began to spin.

Riding the music, black sea devils with glittering eyes spewed from the pipes. As they were puffed into the air, they danced and quivered in a flurry of boney arms and beating wings.

A tremendous wave hit the Prudence broadside, crashing through the salon windows. The room became a swirling vortex as furniture flew with the candlesticks and bottles. Pain claimed her, and the music faded to darkness.

———

Weak light feathered Helen's eyes like a mother's caress. And within its silence, cold smothered the air.

She lay on the sofa. The arctic air traveled freely through broken windows into the salon. Clouds hung low, crushed together, and the ship rested perfectly still in the water.

She covered her eyes against the blinding whiteness everywhere. Helen stood, boots squelching in the soaked carpet, and stepping through slivered glass and shattered wood. The organ remained; undamaged and benign. A remembered shadow whispered in the air.

The unnatural silence amplified her steps and the rustle of her wet clothing. So used to the vigorous swells of the sea, the ship seemed too still. When a note began in the silence, it wavered, joined by the others, gathering to grow and resound.

Helen walked onto the deck and into a world of ice that appeared blue and shadowed for as far as she could see. On the horizon, the starkness blended into the dark skies, ringed with storm clouds.

il Idolin, frozen in the ice, had become a crystal ship. Icicles like spear points dripped from the yardarms and stays. An icy spray of seawater festooned a rope tied to the rail, transforming it into a glacial spider web.

A cold wind blew down from the glaciers, bringing the low guttural growls from the stern. Helen followed a dribble of blood to the rail. The blood led off the deck and across the frozen sea. When she leaned over the side, a trail of crimson widened into a pool where Kinsky lay on his back.

Five wolves ripped at his intestines as they spilled onto the ice, mirroring the entrails of the gutted fish. And like a fish, he still breathed, gasping as one of the wolves stood on his chest and sank fangs deep into his neck, spraying fresh blood that froze mid-air and ribboned their fur like red frosting.

Hovering above Kinsky, the sea devils spun with the music. In a chorus of snarls and growls, the wolves dragged Kinsky's body away from the ship.

Over it all, the music became a crescendo, resounding in the frosty air, then exploding in a cascade of notes that echoed and repeated in undulating waves.

Impaled on the top mast, Captain Godfrey raised sightless eyes toward the frozen sky. Like a swarm of frenzied bees, the sea devils covered his torso, their claws shredding his skin.

il Idolin groaned, shifting in the ice.

"Leviticus, Mrs. Wiggins."

From an open window of the salon, Helen watched the reverend read to Mrs. Wiggins as she knitted, the brass pipes of the organ visible through his body.

"Helen?"

Jim walked toward her, holding twin glasses of frozen champagne. His eyes spoke of eternal love.

She stepped inside, il virgo idolin.

*il virgo idolin; the virgin ghost

Book Club Questions

1. Which story did you feel a connection with? Why did it reso-
nate with you?

2. Do you ever wonder whether there is life out in space? If there is,
what do you think it is like?

3. How well did the stories included meet your expectations for this
anthology?

4. Which story would you have liked to have been longer, or you would
have liked to have had more in-depth involvement with? Why?

5. What did you like the most/least about the anthology? Why?

About the Editor

K ris Cotter lives in Florida with her husband and two loving cats. When she isn't editing, she is reading, crocheting, or watching movies. She also enjoys playing videogames and cooking with her friends.

More books from 4 Horsemen Publications

Anthologies & Collections

4HP Anthologies
Teen Angst: Mix Vol. 1
Teen Angst: Mix Vol. 2
My Wedding Date
The Offices of Supernatural Being
Office Memo 1
The Offices of Supernatural Being
Office Memo 2
The Sentient Space Log Entry 1
The Sentient Space Log Entry 2
Involing Destiny Vol. 1

Demonic Anthologies
Demonic Wildlife
Demonic Household
Demonic Carnival
Demonic Classics
Demonic Vacations
Demonic Medicine
Demonic Workplace
& more to follow!

XXX- Holiday Collection
Unwrap Me
Stuffing My Stocking

Non-Fiction

Jörgen Jensen with Peter Lundgren
Mind Over Tennis: Mastering the Mental Game

Josh Stehle
I Am A Suphero Expert: Growing Up with my Autistic Brother

Kiyomi Holland
HeARTwork

Lael Giebel
Sustainability is for Everyone: Beginning Steps to Creating a Sustainability Program for Your Business

N.B. Johnson
Wonders and Miracles

For Writers

4HP Writer's Resources
The Author's Accountability Planner

Dr. Jenifer Paquette
The General Worldbuilding Guide

Letitia Washington
The Psychology of Character Building for Authors

Megan Mackie
Advanced Con Quest

VALERIE WILLIS
Writer's Bane: Research
Writer's Bane: Formatting 101

ACADEMIA & TEXTBOOKS

DR. JENIFER PAQUETTE & LAURA MITA
Sentence Diagramming 101: Fun with Linguistics (and Movies)

TEXTBOOKS
Composition and Grammar: For HCC by HCC

SCIFI

BRANDON HILL & TERENCE PEGASUS
Between the Devil and the Dark
Wrath & Redemption

PC NOTTINGHAM
Mummified Moon
Severed Squadron

C.K. WESTBROOK
The Shooting
The Collision
The Judgment

T.S. SIMONS
Project Hemisphere
The Space Between
Infinity
Circle of Protection
Sessrúmnir
The 45th Parallel
Orenda

NICK SAVAGE
Us Of Legendary Gods
So We Stay Hidden
The West Haven Undead

TY CARLSON
The Bench
The Favorite
The Shadowless